LYDIA VASSILIADES

SAILING
THE WATERS OF
IOS

A tale of adventure and romance
on the island of Homer

To Zouzouki,
wherever she is

First edition

The cover was designed by Stan Draenos based on an image by macrovector_official using assets from Freepik.com

Translated from the Greek by Stan Draenos

This is a work of fiction. Any resemblance to persons living or dead is coincidental.

The undiscovered country, from whose bourn, no traveler returns

Hamlet

Shakespeare

1

Man is the measure of all things.

Pythagoras

Leaning with all his weight on the handrail of the ship's upper deck, Peter was staring at the horizon, only dimly visible. His wrist was stressed, but he was so abstracted that he didn't notice as he contemplated the Aegean Sea, joined with the sky. He was sitting like a marble figure, afraid that if he moved even a little the magic would be lost. The happiness of the moment was complete. The sun was intense, but the breeze gently cooled his cheeks. The sound of the waters making a wake as the bow of the ship violently cut into the sea accompanied him, lulling him.

It was the end of June and the summer season in the Cyclades had already begun. The sun, a luminous sphere, was at high noon.

"What on earth is Dieter doing all this time?" Peter thought about his friend, who had gone down to the ship's canteen for coffee and sandwiches. "He's taking his time."

His gaze turned for a moment to the side when someone's feet in leather sandals appeared quietly next to him. They belonged, he discovered, to a scrumptious young woman whose blond hair was in pigtails. She stood next to him to watch the vast sea that spread out gracefully before them. But before he had a chance to start up a chat with the woman, Dieter showed up, holding a tray with coffees and two sandwiches in wrappers.

"I was wondering where you were all this time," Peter said frowning.

"There was a long line for coffee, so I had to wait," Dieter answered, slightly miffed and weary from the tedious wait in line. He didn't appreciate the criticism from his friend, who had no idea of conditions at the snack bar.

"I got you a ham and cheese sandwich. It was the simplest thing they had," Dieter remarked, handing it to him. "And here's your espresso."

"Thanks, Dieter!" Peter said with a wry smile.

The two knew each other well from when they were classmates in Hannover, the city where they both were born and raised. Now they were two handsome lads, Dieter thirty-four and Peter thirty-four-and-a-half, both tall, athletic and blond. Peter was a little shorter, with a wide chest and strong legs, as well as edgier and more abrupt than Dieter. He had green eyes and a determined jaw. His hair, falling to his shoulders, was straight and full. By contrast, Dieter was a quiet type, relaxed and measured. Starkly blond, with short, spiked hair. He was bearded, elegant and handsome, with blue eyes and fine features. A straight nose and beautiful lips. Both were physically hardy, being German and programmed for everything or almost everything. From a young age, they hung out a lot since their parents were neighbors and knew each other. Frequent traveling companions, they spent many summer vacations together.

In Hannover, Dieter's family had an antique shop that enjoyed a good clientele and solid reputation. Initially, their competitors had spread some rumors about the authenticity of some items in their collection, but the rumors were debunked and eventually stopped. Dieter was the middle son. He had a younger sister, Petra, and an older brother, Hans, both of whom worked in the antique shop, helping their parents. Besides, the work at the antique shop was enjoyable. Their parents were a conventional, devoted German couple who worked hard to provide the best for their family. They respected their customers and wanted their antique shop to keep its good name. The father had been an accountant before he met Dieter's mother, who had inherited the antique shop from an aunt who had no children. In general, it was a good family, tight-knit and respectable.

Peter's family were entrepreneurs in the restaurant business. His parents had two restaurants and two beer halls, which in fact were profitable enough to ensure a good life for their five-member family. Peter was the middle of three children in the Bower family. He had two sisters, Mia, a year older than he was, and Lisa, his little sister, who was two years younger. He was the only boy. He loved his sisters, but they also adored him. They teased and petted him like their favorite toy. And as a teenager, he always had fun as their escort at parties. Since they were not far apart in age, they gossiped with each other about the flirtations they encountered.

The two friends studied in their home country, but did not pursue their studies too eagerly. Dieter became a graphic designer and worked with some companies, without great enthusiasm in fact, while Peter, after initially studying hotel management, soon realized he had little interest in it and instead he got involved with the sea, which he adored, trying to set up a small yachting business renting pleasure craft. He was just starting out, but he could see that in the yachting sector there was great potential. He had now left behind his cousin Tom, who worked in the office. The trip to the Aegean, and specifically to Ios, where the two friends were headed, was a must for Peter, who meanwhile had infected Dieter with his profound love of the sea. In fact, Peter had organized everything, just as he had promised his friend, taking roughly six months preparing for the trip before their departure.

But this beautiful Cycladic island, close to famed Santorini in the middle of the Aegean, drew Peter's attention for another reason, aside from the marvelous beaches that, in the 1970s, made it a favorite for young tourists. He had heard from an old sailor whom he had met in Hannover three years before, that in the depths of some bay on the island, an ancient shipwreck was to be found, filled with amphorae and two statues. His aged friend adamantly insisted that he had seen it with his own eyes. But, he explained, he had been unable to retrieve the treasure from the depths and had kept totally mum on his finding ever since. For the first time, he was revealing his secret.

2

Dreamer of dreams, born out of my due time

Why should I strive to set the crooked straight?

The Earthly Paradise

William Morris

N ow an elderly, retired yachtsman, Timothy, a skilled skipper, told Peter the story with great conviction. The reason he never returned, he explained, was his wife's illness. For many years, he had to be on hand almost constantly to care of her. Alice had multiple sclerosis and eventually became bedridden. Timothy could now only accept short yachting engagements to nearby ports and lakes. The unfortunate Alice had departed from life three years earlier "but now he was an old man", he explained, and was not able to pursue his quest to retrieve the statues from the shipwreck. It was too late for him, he told Peter, somewhat bitterly. *But he also felt that "it would be a shame for these treasures to remain buried forever."*

He decided to reveal his secret to Peter, who he found very copacetic, having known him for years. Very often, Peter treated him to a beer whenever he showed up in his beer hall. The two of them frequently discussed the magic of the sea and reminisced about their sea cruises, near and far. Peter had confided in him his desire to again visit the Cycladic islands, to swim there in it translucent waters "and to experience God." After many such discussions, and with a few beers more, Timothy decided to tell Peter the story of the shipwreck he had encountered in Ios during one of his trips with German compatriots many, many years ago.

He had to anchor somewhere distant from the shore and he jumped into the water to see if the anchor was well fixed. "The waters there are wonderful, magical, but deep. They descend abruptly. It was wonderfully clear. Such water you have never seen, Peter." He continued his story, lowering his voice and staring Peter in the eyes.

"We were anchored in some deserted cove, in nowheresville, when suddenly, following the long anchor chain, I was astonished to see the remains of an ancient shipwreck appear before me. Fish and sea creatures were swimming around the ancient ship skeleton and then I suddenly noticed amphoras stuck in the deep, as well as the base of a statue. As I was eagerly searching to see what it was, I pumped my flippers to push myself deeper. And there, in the depths, I discovered a well-preserved statue: the statue of a young man with long, strong legs extended fully, one in front and the other a little further back from the first one's heel. His hair was arranged elaborately. His head was remarkable and the whole statue had a unique beauty." He explained that the statue was large, maybe more than one-and-a-half meters tall. Submerged in the sea, its size was hard to estimate, "but for sure it was large. Then I saw another one next to it!"

His breathing decreased, when he realized that he had

made a very important discovery. The shipwreck was indeed ancient. He suspected, he told Peter, that the statues "may have been very, very ancient, maybe even Egyptian". But he could not stay submerged any longer, even though then he was a good swimmer and diver. *"Besides, I also had clients on board the ship. They would be looking for me and wondering why I was taking so long."*

He was forced to surface, he recalled, and get back on the ship, while intending to dive into the water again that afternoon in order to get a better look at what he had seen. However, unfortunately, his plans were totally disrupted since his clients' small daughter had gotten food poisoning from some spoiled nuts she had eaten. They departed quickly for the port of Ios to find a doctor. He had intended, of course, to come back at some point and take his time checking out the shipwreck. But that never happened. Life had other plans for Timothy.

"Now it's too late for all that," he said shaking his head in a worried gesture as Peter listened spellbound. But Peter "was a young man," he told him, and as a young man he as would be able to find what life had denied Timothy. So, half-drunk and pouring out his heart, Timothy revealed to Peter his well-kept secret about the hidden treasure in the depths of lovely Ios. "If you find it, make me a small gift," he said. When Peter asked him if he knew whether, after so many years, the shipwreck had since been found, Timothy declared categorically: "No. It was never found. I kept track of discoveries in the newspapers, but nothing like that was ever reported," he said. And later, when the internet became common, he had made searches. Nothing relevant ever came up. "But who's going to go to that rugged place to drop anchor? You need guts to do that, but back then, I had a long chain for the anchor that made it possible. Only crazy me would do something like that to please my clients. Not that I ever heard any thanks," he added.

3

Prove all things; hold fast that which is good.

New Testament, 1 Thessalonians 5:21

Dieter donned his sunglasses and enjoyed a peaceful coffee. "How great! You were right. Good choice to come to Greece," he said to Peter.

Dieter also loved the sea, but not as much as Peter did. He enjoyed swimming a lot and had also, on certain occasions, done some sailing, mainly with Peter. He liked traveling. But he was also eager to have his own corner of the world, a house with his possessions—books, paintings (he did some art work), fine clothes. He enjoyed as well going to the movies and theater or sometimes to the opera. He wasn't as hooked on money and getting rich as Peter was. He was happy to have enough in order to meet his needs and to enjoy life as he pleased. He was Peter's schoolmate and beloved friend and had a particular weakness for him. Perhaps because his friend was more vigorous, being physically stronger. He made decisions quickly and didn't give up easily once he had made them. He was stubborn, and up to this point, it had served him well.

By contrast, Dieter was more flexible, not so absolute in his judgments, less stubborn and generally more caring about others. Naturally, as a German, he was physically fit, but his character was more easy-going. He was more cultivated, because of the antique shop and his family's history, but also perhaps due to his character. He had a variety of interests. Music was one of his favorite things. He loved playing the flute. His enormous love of music gave him a sense of peace. During his free hours in Hannover, he spent time with his sisters and often with Peter, but also moved in other circles of friends which Peter, oddly, had not gotten to know. He had a lot of interests. He was a graphic artist and had gotten some commissions as a graphic artist, but his main interest was painting.

Recently, when the two of them decided to take a trip to Greece, he started to learn the Greek language and sought out Mary Baumann, who was married to a German, as his language tutor. With her help, he learned enough Greek to at least communicate on basic, everyday matters.

He had some interesting discussions with her about the economic crisis in Greece which had beleaguered the country in recent years. He had read German newspapers that treated Greece as the "bad boy of Europe" and wrote about how corrupt the state was, how it had no choice but to take painful, unpopular measures or else face expulsion from the European Union. Emotionally speaking, he did not embrace these views, which he considered extreme and bordering on racist. He also found fault with these negative press views, from a philosophical point of view.

Ms. Baumann was saddened by the stance of the Germans towards her country and compatriots. She explained to him the tortured path of Greece's historical journey, telling him also about her own experiences. How Greece was devastated by the German occupation during the Second World War and much else.

Naturally, Dieter agreed with her entirely and enjoyed their discussions. In any case, he himself was not ignorant about world affairs and had formed views on European developments and the economic crisis. He often read foreign newspapers, the UK *Guardian* at times, but also the *New York Times.* So he was interested in experiencing for himself what was happening in Greece and how people were getting by, since he had read that they faced lots of serious problems.

"We should have spent more time in Athens, Peter", Dieter told his friend, rolling his eyes. We haven't seen half of the things we said we wanted to see! I wanted to visit Sounion, but we didn't! We should have gone to the Byzantine Museum, which I've read a lot about when it was the villa of the Duchess of Plakentia when she lived in Greece. And there's a lot more we didn't see!"

"Hold off on the complaints, Dieter! We saw a lot of great sights and went to the Acropolis Museum, as well as going up the rock of the Acropolis. We also visited the Benaki Museum, like you wanted, and ate in tavernas in the Plaka neighborhood and elsewhere. Don't forget the Museum of Cycladic Art and the National Gallery. In any case, we'll see more when we get back! So stop complaining and sit down here with me to admire the sea. Tomorrow, we'll discuss our project. Right now, I want to have a clear mind. In any case, you said it too. I've thought about a lot of problems we might encounter along the way. But I've figured out alternatives for most of them."

"The studio you rented is at the port, right? Maybe you should have rented something in the main town instead?"

"No, the port is better. It's right on the sea. No hills. It has tavernas for food and everything we need to buy for our treasure hunt. In any case, Timothy urged us to stay there. So let's stay there for now. Once we get things organized, we can move somewhere else," Peter said.

He began to get impatient with Dieter, who had lots of questions about his grand scheme, something that would make him rich! Of course, Peter was already well off, but he also was in pursuit of the adrenalin rush! He wanted to find the hidden treasure. As much as wanting the money, he wanted to prove to himself that he could do it.

Still, what he hadn't included in his plan was what he would do with his findings, if and when he managed to raise them from the sea. How legal was what they were doing and how could he market the treasure? Furthermore, what kinds of dangers would they face?

But for Peter, all of that was what they call small whoop. Because Peter was an enthusiast and, while organized, he was also reckless when it came to issues of law and legality. Dieter had seen examples of this in Peter's loose adherence to the rules in other circumstances.

Dieter thought to himself that, despite Peter's stubbornness, his ideas would soon fall apart. He didn't think much would come of Peter's plan, but that didn't bother him. In reality, he had gone along with Peter for the trip, for the experience, for the fun of it, for an adventure if nothing else. He didn't believe a word of Timothy's story or how likely it was that they would find those statues, but go tell Peter that. Peter's stubbornness was proverbial. He always persisted, even when things turned out differently than he expected. Even then, he would not accept things immediately. He would try to manipulate matters to get what he wanted.

Dieter didn't bring up the issue of their room rental again. *"In the end, summer in Greece was magnificent wherever you were,"* he thought to himself.

4

I am not an Athenian or a Greek,

but a citizen of the world.

Socrates, as quoted by Plutarch

The boat reached the port of Ios. It was a lively place, with white-canopied tavernas and interesting shops. People were waiting for the boat to arrive. They were lined up with their colorful suitcases as they waited for the ship to tie up so the passengers could disembark and those waiting could board.

Near the entrance to the harbor was a small, whitewashed church with an impressive dome and a bell tower. It stood on a flat area near some rocks, and immediately caught the attention of Dieter, who tried to take a photograph with his mobile phone. He looked up and saw Chora, the main town, built upon the hill beyond the port. He was moved by the charm of the scene. "Peter, look!" he said, pointing to brilliantly white village atop the hill. At the peak was a small chapel and next to it a palm tree. Magical!

People hastily got off the ship and swarmed the port, carrying their backpacks and suitcases, eager to start their island vacation. After asking a local, Peter and Dieter located the studio apartment that they had rented. They headed there quickly and, after making the necessary arrangements with the owner and receiving the keys, they entered the studio. It was a fairly large room, clean and well-appointed. It had two beds and a table with two chairs, complementing the furnishings. The beds were rather narrow, but that didn't bother them. It was standard. On a shelf was a small flat-screen television. In the kitchenette were two cups and a coffeemaker. Also a microwave oven, as well as four plates, four glasses and some silverware.

"Congrats to Ios! A coffeemaker and cups. Amidst crisis and suffering, an espresso machine? Right!" Peter said.

"What did you expect, Peter? For people to be more destitute? Here we are on an island in the middle of the Aegean. Do you think they are rich capitalist industrialists?" an agitated Dieter answered. "The people of the island are making efforts to make our visit enjoyable, even by providing us with this espresso machine." Peter nodded, but didn't answer.

After a while, they both stretched out on their beds, suddenly overcome by fatigue from their trip. Later, they emerged from the room to take a walk along the harbor, where people strolling at that hour. They sat at a taverna and ordered beers, a Greek salad and French fries. They finished their meal with watermelon, which smelled of summer and, according to Peter, was "excellent". Finally, they decided to get up from the table and go back to their room, where they immediately fell asleep. They would begin to execute their program the next day, along with their holiday proper.

5

I understand the large hearts of heroes,
The courage of present times and all times.

Leaves of Grass

Walt Whitman

A ndreas was a loner. He had become embittered due to the loss of his wife, who he loved dearly. She was the woman of his life. His family was a well-off Athenian family and he had been living a good life, until he "struck an iceberg", as a good friend of his put it. His dear companion, his wife, the person who understood him and offered unqualified love, had fallen seriously ill and died within a year.

Deeply wounded, his heart ached. He was still among the living while she was in a damp, dark tomb. He couldn't bear the thought of her in a state of decay. So many things had happened in the years since her absence. Many new buildings had been built, new movies produced, and he had travelled to many places, places she would never see. The economic crisis arrived, people suffered terribly, unemployment and misfortune plagued the country, but she was absent. Time has ceased for her. Mortality had called.

Years passed, but the pain remained. He wasn't able to listen to Rachmaninoff, the great composer and pianist, because it reminded him of his wife. She loved his music enormously and listened to it incessantly. Was her illness caused by the use of her mobile phone and maybe the computer? The doctors gave him no satisfactory answer. "No, we don't think so," they told him. "If that were so, all of us would have gotten sick." Eventually, he came to believe that it likely was the Chernobyl nuclear accident. His wife had taken a swim in the sea during the days of the accident. No one knew at that moment that a nuclear accident had taken place and that the radioactive cloud had already reached Greece, polluting the waters. The former Soviet Union kept the accident secret. It became public when the Swedes discovered it. Meanwhile, the damage had been done. Now, those who had departed, his wife included, had paid the price.

At some point, he decided to leave Athens and settle in Ios. He believed that there he could ease his sorrow. The sun, the sea, the Cycladic breezes, the white houses and waves comforted him. He loved Ios where he had gone many times as a youth, when it was in fashion and all the hippies in Europe and America gathered there every year from the spring until October. He hoped that he would be able to forget. But he was bitterly disappointed. He thought about her every day and carried on a dialogue with Athena, asking her questions and seeking answers.

In Ios, the island of Homer, he had gotten to know some likeable people who, with their warmth and innocence, somehow eased the pain within him. He preferred living there to breathe the clean air rather than stay in Athens, with its pollution and daily hassles. He had some money to get by, despite the costs involved in the course of Athena's tragedy. He was now over fifty, but in good shape, since he walked regularly and watched his diet. He believed that the factors that were most responsible for physical decline were stress and worry. So he avoided them as much as possible. Aside from that, he was a handsome, olive-skinned, dark-haired man with a good physique and, by Greek standards, tall.

He had studied architecture at the Polytechnic University, but, after Athina's death, ceased working. Work, in fact, had taken up a lot of his time, reducing the time he spent with Athina. Naturally, he did not know that she would depart so quickly, so young, nor could he have even imagined it.

In Ios, he had started a bar that opened when he felt like it. It didn't have any employees. He started the business mainly to keep himself occupied and avoid thinking too much. Naturally, that turned out to be a futile hope and he almost immediately saw that he would always be thinking about her, even when he was serving a customer. It was as if he lived in a parallel universe.

In the winter, he barely worked at all. He closed the bar. During the three months of summer, however, he had plenty of business. He liked that. He wasn't particularly interested in making money. He needed just enough to live, without craziness. Without exaggeration. "Besides, what could I do... What am I after? I don't want anything except peace of mind," he thought.

Beyond that, his life was uneventful, maybe even boring, one could say. However, he had gotten used to life on the island and was content. He didn't ask for anything more. He didn't want disruptive events or tense situations. Of these, he had had an overdose. "Enough, no more drama," he thought.

He had good feelings about other permanent residents who, like him, had settled in Ios and operated businesses. Two male friends and one female, an Italian. In truth, all he wanted was just peace and quiet. Nor did he want to talk about his misfortune and loneliness. The abandonment that beset his life and ravaged him. What can anyone say? he thought. How to explain to others the feeling that overwhelms you, that turns you to stone, that freezes you? How can they understand you if they have not lived it. And why drag them into the darkness of your own thoughts? He tried to appear calm and at ease, despite the fact that he was suffering inside. He, and only he, knew what it would mean to live his whole life with the images of his wife's loss, with their conversations, with the image of her lying dead, covered with a purple sheet.

With his friends on the island, in any case, he tried to be sociable. During the winter, they made some delicious meals and regularly dined together. Every so often, they played backgammon. One of them, Antonis, was a little older than he was and had a shop with herbs and local products, as well as popular gift items. He was a wonderful flute and baglama player, but also played the harmonica. He often entertained them with his music. A handsome man with tousled, brown hair and an impressive beard, he was also of good character. He had lived permanently on the island for fifteen years, initially together with his wife, but later they split. He was in a relationship with a local girl, Maria, who was very congenial and worked with her parents in a family business, a small hotel.

The third member of the circle, Haris, a former attorney, was no longer professionally active, wrote poetry and, in any case, presented himself to others as a poet, adding that he was working on a novel. Haris was very cultivated and talented. He had been living there alone for some time. His girlfriend, a lovely redhead, had left him suddenly when she found a younger man and, in a flash, had fallen in love with him, taking off for Wales with her new love. At first, that troubled him, but, with the help of friends, he appeared to get over it and, at this point, was devoting himself to his writing. He put on some weight, but his charismatic personality compensated for the few extra kilos. He was of average height, blond with bright blue eyes and had just turned 55.

Finally, the fourth person in the group was an Italian woman from Calabria named Carla, who worked at the reception desk of a good hotel. She had been living in Ios for years and liked it. She went back to her homeland only every four years or so, even though Italy was close by. A beautiful woman around 40 years of age, maybe a bit older, she was awesomely stylish, with straight long brown hair and green eyes. Those eyes betrayed a certain melancholy, even when she laughed. She wasn't very open and spoke little of her past, nor did she like getting a lot of questions about it, finessing those on the island who indiscreetly asked her about personal issues. She had a friend from Switzerland, Andy, and had recently split up with him, seemingly permanently. She hadn't opened up about her feelings, but her friends understood that the break-up had bothered her. She had a mania for photography and took some exceptional photographs with the Nikon camera she rarely parted with. In Italy, she had a younger sister who she spoke with regularly on the phone. Her parents had died, she told her friends.

These then were the members of Andreas' circle of friends on Ios. They regularly had great discussions, mainly during the winter when they spent more time together. They cooked all sorts of delicious meals, and in fact, were good cooks. Carla cooked spaghetti with different sauces, as well as with seafood and tuna along with a number of other Italian dishes. She also had a talent for cooking vegetables, that she loved, while the men were more skilled with fish and meat.

The four of them imbibed good wine and passed the time happily, with Haris reciting his own poems, as well as those of other poets, and with Antonis playing music on his flute. Their times together were relaxed and trouble-free, infused with a sense of mutual affection and congeniality. Rivalries were absent. All of them had a good sense of humor, and the everyday happenings on the island gave them lots of fodder for gossip.

Politically speaking, they were all on the same wavelength,

with a few minor differences. You could say they each had their own political opinions, but without ideological fixations. To the positive deeds they witnessed, they reacted approvingly. Generally, all of them had a critical spirit and a sophisticated political sensibility. They were particularly concerned with Turkish aggressiveness that was growing year by year, and naturally, they were shaken when they learned about Turkish air space violations in the Aegean.

Still, they lived on Ios and enjoyed the island's beauty, the sun and the sea. The three of them lived in Chora, the main town, while Carla was temporarily staying at the hotel where she worked a little outside the town. After her break-up, she left the wonderful villa that she had rented with Andy and was looking to buy a place in Chora.

6

A man who knows the price of everything
and the value of nothing.
Lady Windemere's Fan
Oscar Wilde

Peter drank his coffee as he gazed out at the sea. A wonderful breeze, divine and restorative, wafted across his face as the day began to heat up. His friend had gone to shop for some goods at the mini-mart and bakery for their breakfast, but hadn't come back yet. He thought about the venture he was planning, wondering if he would succeed. He, of course, had done preparatory work in Hannover and was clear about what needed to be done. He had located the equipment they would need for their underwater dive and also found an inflatable dinghy to rent. In the coming days, he would be on site to arrange for everything. But beforehand, he would explore by land to get as close as possible to the place Timothy indicated. One way or another, he would rent a car. For the time being, they had not moved from the port except to take the small bus to the brilliantly white village of Chora. In any case, they were on vacation. At least that is how it would appear to others. But there also was some truth to it. They were holidaying on this wonderful island with its enchanting colors and fragrances from the thyme that blossomed even in the crevices of rocks. Aromas, small flowers of rose and purple next to the sea and the rocks, white buildings, golden beaches with crystal blue waters and marvelous sunsets.

One afternoon they went to Chora and sat for a coffee at the square and did some people-watching. It was very pleasant. Then they took a stroll through the narrow lanes and went up to the village of Milos. The view was stunning. The water, like a blue carpet, spread out before them. It felt as if they were in a magical land. Afterwards, they slowly descended toward the village and sat at a taverna. They ordered a Greek salad and French fries, as well as a local sour cheese that the taverna owner had recommended. It turned out to be truly incredible. Darkness slowly descended, making Chora extremely beautiful. As soon as it got dark, they went to a little bar, very charming, and drank some cold beer.

They returned relatively early to the port and stopped nearby for another beer. They liked the island greatly, as least what they had seen so far. For a swim, they had gone on foot nearby, just past a white chapel, to some flat rocks and a beach with clean waters. Timothy had mentioned the place to Peter and he was right. Once they had gotten a car, they would also go for a swim near the port and at Koubara to a beautiful beach a bit further on and, of course, to Mylopotas, as well as to the divine Manganari, at some distance at the other end of the island. With the inflatable dinghy they would be able to explore other places, beneath the sea, as they had planned.

The island was wonderful. The water remarkable, clean and crystalline. All around the view was enchanting. As for food, everything they had tried so far was excellent. They had eaten fish and greens at the port and, on another occasion, a Greek specialty: stewed eggplant with potatoes and squash. "This is called briam," they were told.

Dieter followed Peter's instructions regarding the program. He had no objections. He followed patiently until he exploded. Because now and again, that happened. Not often. But every few years, there was some tension between them. Still, they had been close friends from their youth and so he let those moments go. In any case, Dieter had a low-key personality. He wasn't into drama and angry words. He avoided arguments.

Peter seemed certain about the program they would follow. He had made the plans and, in this respect, he was unquestionably skilled. Anyway, on their past trips, he had done the organizing, and indeed masterfully, planning their activities so that they could both see sights worth visiting and have a good time. On this, the two friends were in agreement. They were on the same page.

Naturally, on the plans to search for the treasure, Dieter didn't make any suggestions, since he was almost certain that it was all a pointless caper. *Let Peter think what he wants, he told himself. Let's not shatter the tall story which he had come to believe. In any case, what would it add to the discussion if I told him it was all BS? What would I add to the situation? He would just get angry and would start a fight. Without reason or cause. If he wants to believe this nonsense, then fine. Let him believe it. When he realizes there is nothing to it, he will come back to his senses, like it or not. Never mind. We will get in some swimming and have our holiday. It's summer, he thought. Time for a good time.*

7

There is a lady sweet and kind,
Was never face so pleased my mind,
I did but see her passing by,
And yet I love her till I die.

There is a Lady

Barnabe Googe

The day after their jaunt to Chora, Peter suggested going for a swim to Mylopotas, which, he had read, had an enormous beach. Timothy had told him that he had gone there back in the day and found it terrific. In fact, he had told him that then—in the 1970s—at the far end of the beach was a little restaurant that rented some simple rooms for a good price. He had often stayed there. Naturally, this was before he got involved with being a skipper. In any case, he had spoken to him ardently about the beauty of the beach which now was no longer virgin territory like it was then, since now it was a camping site and had some hotels, beach bars and the rest. Yet it was so big that it didn't get crowded. "Not to mention that it had fine gravel, so that the sand didn't get into your pants!" Timothy added with a smile.

Peter had found all this on the Web, as he often did before visiting somewhere. "An enormous beach! And very beautiful. Let's go today," he told Dieter. A little later, they went there by taxi. It was a short distance away but they weren't up for taking the bus. In fact, they were there in half an hour and paid the taxi driver, who agreed to come back to pick them up later in the day. They went down to the beach and found a place that they were happy with. Spreading out their beach mats and colorful towels, they started out with some tanning under the burning sun.

Dieter, who was the more sensitive of the two, had brought along a small sun umbrella. He opened it and planted it in the sand. They put their things in the shade. In a while, Peter joined him, having gotten overheated in the hot sun.

They took their swims in the crystalline waters, read their books—Dieter reading a novel and Peter a crime thriller—and then moved on to a nearby beach bar to down some ice-cold beers. Just what they needed to quench their thirst. They stayed at the beach bar for some time and discussed soberly how they would carry out their ambitious plan. In reality, however, Peter was instructing Dieter on how they would move forward with the plan. He had already found where they could rent an inflatable dinghy. It would be cheap, but that wasn't a problem. They had plenty of cash with them.

After discussing the details exhaustively as they sat under the thatched awning, then paid for the beers and went back to the beach. Later, around 6 o'clock, after a final swim, they called the taxi driver who arrived promptly for the return trip.

In their room, worn out from the sea, they took showers and stretched out on their beds. Around 8 o'clock, they hadn't dressed yet, but the heat had abated. They sat out on their quiet veranda and drank some espressos. They talked about the beach at Mylopotas, which had been delightful. Slowly, darkness descended. The sea before them was unreal. Such beauty!

They decided to dine by going up to Chora, which had impressed them enormously. After dressing, they emerged from the room and locked the wooden door behind them. They walked uphill by foot, taking the stairs that led directly to the village. It wasn't far and, in any case, they wanted to get a little exercise. In Chora, they found some taverna. Sitting at a table, they ordered two roasted chicken dishes and salads, local cheese and half a kilo of white wine.

Across from them, sitting alone, was a beautiful woman with green, almond-shaped eyes. She seemed abstracted and totally absorbed in her thoughts. She barely touched her food. At one moment, her gaze encountered Dieter's. He was looking at her intently, since her appearance reminded him of a Renaissance beauty, like that of a Botticelli, a connection evoked by his fondness for works of art.

"Lovely," he thought. "A girl of unique beauty." He mumbled something to Peter whose back was turned to her, leaving her out of his range of vision.

Shortly later, the beautiful woman paid her bill and left the restaurant. Dieter followed her with his eyes as she stepped softly away. She was petite, with long brown hair. She reminded him of a graceful antelope.

"That was a beautiful woman," he told Peter.

"Well, you'll see plenty of beautiful women here. The place is full of them," Peter answered, nodding his head. And adding: "In Mylopotas there were lots of them where we sat down."

"For sure, but this one had something special. A delicacy, a finesse. Wonderful eyes…a charming gait."

"So how did you manage to see all that? Bravo, Dieter! Don't worry, though. We'll find something for you. This one or some other gazelle," Peter told his friend teasingly.

After the meal, the two took a stroll through the village.

They saw little shops with tourist goods, sandals and handbags hung outside. They dawdled for a while. Dieter was interested in buying some sandals, but he couldn't decide what he liked, so he left it for later.

Going further on, they spotted a nice bar. Some beautiful music was coming out of it. From the guitars, they recognized the sounds of Al Di Meola, John McLaughlin, and Paco De Lucia. Peter proposed going in for a drink, since it was still too early to head for bed. Dieter agreed. They went in and sat at a table. At the bar, the woman Dieter had noticed earlier in the restaurant was sitting chatting with the bartender. Noticing her immediately, he nudged his friend.

"Take a look, Peter. There she is, the woman I saw before! The one I told you about. She is sitting at the bar talking to the bartender. Check her out!"

"OK, Dieter," Peter turned and cast an inquisitive eye on the woman. "Mmm. She's nice, but isn't she a little old? She seems so."

"What are you saying? Are you serious?" Dieter answered in a low, slightly irritated voice. "She's lovely...she has style. She has beautiful eyes, but it's hard to tell in this bad lighting," he said defensively.

"Alright, then. Let's not have an argument about a woman," Peter answered casually. "What'll you have? I say a Jameson whiskey. You?"

"I think I'll have a Mochito." Dieter got up and went directly to the bar to order the drinks, taking the occasion to see the woman who had drawn his attention. He made the order and waited to receive the drinks. The woman turned her head and gave him a quick glance. Then, she turned in the other direction and started looking for something in her purse.

The drinks were ready. Dieter thanked the bartender, took the drinks and returned to their table.

"Whoa, Peter. I really like her," he said.

"Are you nuts, Dieter? We just got here and you found something to occupy yourself? We have to focus on work, not on romantic adventures. We talked about all that. You have to focus on the goal. Otherwise, if your mind is elsewhere, we're not going to get anything done. But I noticed that it's been a long time since you've said anything about anyone in Hannover. Were you waiting until we got here for someone to attract you? You make me wonder!" Peter said.

"OK. Don't be so negative. I'm just saying I like her. I won't bring up the subject again."

"That's fine, Dieter. End of conversation," Peter said with a note of irritation.

Dieter turned to his thoughts, without sharing them with his friend. After the first drink, Dieter decided to go for a second. Not that this was his habit, but now he had a reason to do so. He was again at the bar to order the drink, but his real purpose was to see the beautiful woman better from up close. The bartender and the woman were talking in a low voice and at some moment laughed. Dieter didn't want to interrupt their conversation and waited patiently until the bartender noticed him. That came a few minutes later. "Another Mochito, please!" he declared.

The bartender got busy fixing the drink, giving Dieter the chance to cast his eyes on the woman, who apparently didn't notice his attention. The drink was ready and Dieter went back to his friend.

Suddenly, a group of young people entered the bar and the atmosphere livened up. Commotion, laughter and shouting. After a while, the two friends got up, paid and left. They took the footpath back down to the port. Back home, Peter fell into bed like a log and fell immediately asleep. Soon, he began snoring.

Dieter was asleep for about five minutes when his friend's snoring woke him up. He went out on the veranda and plopped down into a lounge chair. Gazing out at the view, thoughts of the woman from the taverna churned in his head. "She was really beautiful. Who knows...was she Greek? She didn't look Greek. Was she on vacation? Maybe she was a friend of the bartender, since they showed some familiarity between them. Or maybe even she was the bartender's wife. End of story," he thought. Her image kept him awake, but eventually, he dozed off. He was still on the veranda when dawn broke.

8

As a small child,

I felt in my heart two contradictory feelings,

the horror of life and the ecstasy of life.

My Heart Laid Bare

Charles Baudelaire

Andreas rose from bed feeling blue. He had stayed up late the previous night and hadn't gotten enough sleep. But he had to get up right away to go to his shop, where he was expecting beverage and wine deliveries. The last boat had not brought enough product to supply all the shops, but now his turn had come. He went to the kitchen to make himself a coffee. Then he dressed and, after drinking his coffee, ate two pieces of toast with cheese, took some cash and his credit card and left home.

After finishing what he had to do in the wine cellar, he telephoned his friend Antonis, who was at his nearby shop. He proposed going for coffee and a chat.

Antonis still had some work to do, so he suggested that Andreas drop by his place. In any case, "it was still early," he said.

"Come on by and we will go later." Andreas agreed. Finally, he went by Antony's shop and they sat and chatted for some time. He had a need to talk to a friend. For some days, he had not been feeling well. He was again caught up in thinking about his lost wife and what had happened, bringing him down, as often happened. "I see old women 100 years old on the street, and Athina is not alive. Isn't that unjust? I know it's not good for me to say this, but it just pops up in my mind."

"The point my friend is that you did whatever you could. Don't keep tormenting yourself...enough is enough!"

"I know. You're right. But I miss her and what happened was unfair. Unjust, a shame, tragic and whatever else you can say. A young woman with no family medical history!"

The two men agreed that, rather than go for a coffee, they would meet again that evening. Antonis closed shop at 8 o'clock and Andreas would open the bar at 9:30, so they agreed to get together for a bite to eat that evening at a taverna they both liked. Their rendezvous was for 8. "I'll also call Haris to see if he wants to come and find us there," Antonis said, adding that it would be good if Carla came too. "It's been a couple of days since I've seen her. How is she?"

"She's fine. I saw her a few days ago and we sat and talked a while at the bar one evening. She has some issues, of course, with the move she has to make as soon as she can find the right place. From what I understand, she has some issues with Andy, who left her—in any case, it cost her—but also with her sister. I'm not exactly sure. She didn't go into details. Aside from that, we had a few laughs over happenings at the hotel and some of the bizarre requests being made by the tourists."

"Yeah, I figured something was going on, but I didn't ask. If she wanted to, she should tell me herself. Anyway, I'm happy she is generally OK. I'll call her to see if she can come, unless she's working."

"Great. We pick it up tonight. Right now, I need to get

going and let you work. You have customers. I'm gone. This evening. If something changes, let me know."

Andreas headed home. He decided to make a stop at a mini-mart to do some shopping. He needed a few things for breakfast. He was out of coffee, tea and few other things. Later at home, he again saw the news on the TV and shook his head at the disheartening new political developments and the economic misery in general. He took a shower, he eagerly ate a "poor, but honest" plate of bread and cheese (*psomotiri*) and fell into bed to sleep, being very tired.

He woke up in the afternoon, this time in a good mood. The sleep had revived him. He turned on the TV to see the news again and then fixed his afternoon coffee. Sitting on his bed drinking coffee and watching the news, he didn't see anything new and looked out the window at the blue sky. What beauty! Little birds were flying and chirping near his window.

What a shame that Athina is not here to see it. What a shame...but no. He shouldn't again have thoughts like that. He pushed her out of his thoughts. Not again. No. He shouldn't get caught up again in that abyss of dark emotions. He couldn't change anything about Athina's fate and the course of his relationship with her. Unless he were able to make a trip in some time machine and managed to change the outcome of events. But that is impossible, he realized. As they say, the only things sure in life are death and taxes.

Time was passing and he had to get ready for the rendezvous with his friends and then afterwards to open up his little bar. Emerging from his thoughts, he dressed quickly, leaving his place and walking quickly to the taverna where he would find the rest of his companions as planned.

The evening was very pleasant, with the four friends dining together at the taverna that they all liked. Haris recited lines from a poem that was popular those days while Carla was in a good mood and told jokes about different crazy things that happened at the hotel, with its weird guests who often made totally unreasonable requests. They then laughed a lot about an event that was truly a joke. One of the clients, a well-known female singer, had singed her hair with the curler that she was using to style it. Panicky, she tried to find a wig so that she could go without causing an uproar in the hotel! The story distracted Andreas, enabling him to emerge from his sorrow at least for a while. Later, he left to open his business in a good mood.

9

A man must eat a peck of salt with his friend

before he knows him.

Don Quixote

Cervantes

Peter revved up the outboard motor. The dinghy headed out. The two friends were going for their first trip with the inflatable craft Peter had rented after first securing diving equipment. He had done everything on his own, telling Dieter he "had it all organized."

They planned to explore some bays to the north, relatively close to the port. In one of those, Timothy had told Peter, he had seen the shipwreck. He didn't remember if it was the third, fourth or fifth cove, since many years had passed, but it was a rocky bay, without good anchorage. Unable to get close to the shore, Timothy had cast anchor near the mouth of the cove.

Dieter listened somewhat indifferently to what Peter was

saying. It was enough for him that they would be swimming every day in clear, crystalline waters.

The sun had begun shining intensely as they departed from the port. The dinghy gliding across the sea like a kite. The waters foamed noisily. They reached a small bay and Peter found a good place to drop anchor. As soon as he had tied up the raft, he put on his wetsuit and oxygen tanks with Dieter's help and did the same for Dieter. He plunged into the water to begin exploring. Shortly afterwards, Dieter followed. The water was wonderfully clean, chilly but superb. They made a familiarization trip, exploring the depths in careful detail. They saw fish and octopi underneath the rocks and places with seaweed. But nothing they saw suggested a shipwreck. After a long search, they came up with nothing.

Growing tired, they emerged from the sea and climbed onto the dinghy. Peter, who had bought an air-powered speargun, decided to dive back into the water, hoping to catch a fish. His idea about fish was rewarded. He was in fact lucky, catching a huge black seabream. It was almost three kilos heavy, he estimated. He would take it to the taverna to be grilled, he told Dieter to his delight.

At 5:30 pm, they raised anchor, took off their wetsuits and started their return trip. The sun was still blazing and after so many hours without shade they were feeling dizzy. They were Germans and well-exercised, *but the sun was hot.* Strangely, the port was quiet. Finding a place to dock, they carefully tied up the dinghy, gathered their things and were soon heading on foot to their room, which was only a few minutes away.

10

To do injustice is more disgraceful than to suffer it.

Georgias

Plato

C arla was standing behind the reception desk at the small hotel where she worked looking at the computer. Today they had new arrivals and she was swamped with work. A group of rambunctious young Italians from Modena showed up. Happy to have arrivals that spoke her native language, she was also found their unruly jabbering and laughing tiresome.

The hotel was a fine place, with a remarkable view and, of course, a swimming pool, despite its location close to the beach. In any case, all of the hotels in Ios now had swimming pools. In recent years, many tourist compounds and accommodations had been built and had nothing to envy other island destinations. Beyond the new compounds, that without exaggeration were beautiful, Ios offered numerous remarkably beautiful beaches, with crystal clear, transparent water, distinctive island architecture, and high-quality cuisine using local products, like its famous cheeses, as well as the enchanting Aegean Sea. It was a beautiful island and, for that reason, tourists preferred it over many other places in the world.

Carla's preoccupation with the Italian arrivals was interrupted by the ring of the telephone. Answering, she heard the voice of her sister on the other end of the line calling from Italy. Her sister, Gratsiella, was four years younger and almost always involved in some kind of misadventure. Most recently, she had an issue with her former companion, Giovani, who had abused her physically before abandoning her, throwing her television set out the window in anger, after extracting from her 80,000 euros, which was her share from the sale of her mother's estate. "I made the mistake of putting him on my account and he went and withdrew the money without my knowing it. He didn't say anything, of course. When I noticed, it was too late," she told Carla. Generally speaking, Gratsiella had demonstrably bad taste in men. As Carla told her, to little effect, she was a poor judge of character and tended to be attracted to problematic figures. If the other person did not have a behavior problem, she wasn't interested!

Gratsiella, of course, made the excuse that "in the beginning, he was good", but she had been deceived. Now once more she was seeking her sister's help to get her out of a fix. Her rent was overdue and, along with unpaid bills, she owed around 8000 euros.

"It's the same story every time, Gratsiella. This can't go on. You have to be extra careful about who you let in your house and who you lend money to. What do you mean you were sorry for him? Did you get to know him that well after three months? It drives me wild that you are so naïve. You need also to find another job, something that pays better than the one you have. You have the skills. You know languages. English and a little French. For sure you can find something better than the shop you work at, which doesn't pay you much or regularly.

"I know, Carla. You're right, but…I messed up. I know it and I am ashamed. It's the last time, I promise you, I won't drag you into my problems again, I swear," she told her sister in a sad voice.

"OK. I've heard that many times. I can send you six thousand right now, because I'm a little short myself. Please, use it well. Pay off your bills immediately. I have expenses here and, as you know, I'm planning to move. I've got a lot on my plate. Anyway, I'll send you the other two thousand next month. That's all I can do right now. Please get it together and sober up. As for Giovani, find a lawyer and file a suit to get your money back, if you can. What can I say? I'm very sorry to hear your news. But it seems you still haven't gotten your head on straight."

"That's so great, Carla. Many thanks. I'll wait for you to send me the six thousand. Please do it quickly. And thanks again!"

The phone call ended, leaving Carla feeling peeved. The same old story. Her sister was thoughtless. Flighty. But it had always been like this. Their mother had managed to keep her somewhat in line. But since her passing, Gratsiella became much worse. The height of her stupidity (what else can you call it) was when, at the age of twenty-two, she was caught in possession of the drug ecstasy. It took her a while to get through what followed. Lawyers, trials, police, and so on. She ended up doing time. It was a dark page in Carla's family history that she avoided thinking about. She had suffered a lot from her sister's problems. And now Gratsiella had gone off-track again, she thought angrily. Worse, she had serious doubts that she was being told the truth. The whole truth.

As soon as her shift ended, a weary Carla went straight to her room and stretched out in bed to relax. She didn't want to eat or talk with anyone. She wanted to hide under the sheets and unwind. The day before, she had agreed before to meet up with Antonis and Andreas in the evening and go for a bite to eat at their favorite taverna. The thought comforted her. She closed her eyes and Morpheas soon took her gently under his magical wings.

11

Do I contradict myself?

Very well,then, I contradict myself.

I am large, I contain multitudes.

Song of Myself

Walt Whitman

Peter and Dieter were sitting on the veranda gazing out at the sea, which was changing colors as the sun set over the Aegean. As darkness began to descend, they got up to get ready to go to the village to eat.

"Should we take the fish with us? What say you?" Dieter asked his friend.

"Yes, of course. We should."

"Great. Go ahead and wrap it in aluminum foil."

When they finished wrapping up the fish, the two friends locked up and left the apartment. The bus had just arrived. Boarding at the last minute, they were soon headed up to the village.

The night was sweet and the temperature had dropped.

Arriving at the popular taverna, Peter went in to find the owner to arrange grilling the fish. He ordered other dishes, since he wanted to try out the food, but also to accompany the fish with greens, a Greek salad, beets, eggplant salad, two orders of French fries, unresinated white wine and olives.

They were eating the fish Peter had caught enthusiastically when two men, who appeared to be Greek, sat down next to them. Dieter recognized the barman from the place that they visited the other day. The Greeks commented on the huge fish that the two Germans were eating. The taverna-owner appeared in good order and the two men asked if he was serving fish. "No," was the answer. "That one was caught by our two friends here, and I grilled it for them since it was still early and it wasn't crowded," the man said, nodding with a smile towards the two Germans, who realized that the conversation was about their fish. Peter, in a moment of generosity, offered to the men some of the fish—half of it, in fact—since "it is a lot for us and it would be a shame for it to go to waste." And so it happened.

That's how the two Germans met Andreas and Antonis while, a short time later, Carla showed up! It was the woman who had drawn Dieter's attention a few days before. The atmosphere was agreeable. The two German friends explained how much they liked the island. It was the first time they had visited Ios, but earlier, when they were kids, they had gone to Rhodes with their parents, as well as to Crete, while three years ago they both had visited Santorini and Mykonos. For their part, their Greek interlocutors told them what was worth seeing on Ios which, among other things, was rumored to be the island where Homer was buried.

Carla, the Italian, asked how long they planned to stay, and where. She told them about the hotel on the route to Mylopotas where she worked. For his part, Dieter was overjoyed by this chance encounter and, betraying his feelings, couldn't take his eyes off Carla. The five talked incessantly. Antonis treated the

Germans to wine and Andreas the fruit that followed the meal. Carla also seemed to be having a good time.

Things moved along happily for nearly two hours until Andreas said he had to leave to open his bar because "time had passed." He invited them all to drop by later for a drink. Dieter was delighted and Peter, pleased by the positive comments about the fish he had caught, was relaxed and cheerful, without rough edges. Overall, it was an unusually interesting get-together, even more so for Dieter. Eventually, the group—for a group they had become—paid the bill and got up to leave. They decided to all go to Andreas' bar together.

Going through the narrow lanes of the village, the sounds of a guitar reached their ears. Then they saw that a blond man with a beard, looking like a Viking, who was sitting on a small walkway strumming his guitar and singing in broken Greek:

Echoun rixi paraga-di

Sas aresi i Ella-da Miss,

Ti tha ka-nete to vradi,

Do you like, Mamazelle the Greece!*

Both the guitarist and his song were terrific. The four, along with other passers-by, paused for some time to listen. A while later, at Andreas' bar, they all sat together, and carried on a loud, but friendly discussion. Dieter was focused on Carla and Peter talked to Andreas and Antonis about music and bar-life, since he himself, as he told them, was in the profession and, in fact, owned two bars in Hannover!

They carried on for some time and split up after first exchanging compliments and phone numbers. The two German took some stairs to go down to the port, while Antonis left with Carla, taking her to the hotel in his automobile.

Despite being tired, Dieter was feeling elated and unable to sleep, since he had just met a woman who attracted him enormously. He was so worked up that he walked back and forth between the veranda and the room speaking incessantly to Peter, who had stretched out, since he was dead tired.

"So once again you're a lucky man, Dieter! You found the woman you liked. But what on earth were you talking about all the time!" he asked his friend laughingly.

"We talked about all sorts of things, about Italy, about painting. She said she had studied Fine Arts. We talked about Ios, how she ended up there and lots more. It was great. Congrats, Peter, for the fish! Let's go catch another one!"

Peter didn't hear what he was saying. He was already snoring.

*Not knowing Greek, the singer has fun winging it.

12

I dreamt that I dwelt in marble halls,

with vassals and serfs at my side.

The Bohemian Girl

Alfred Bunn

T he next day, the two Germans headed out again on their dinghy along the same side of the island they visited before. This time, they ventured to the next cove and took a swim in the brilliantly blue waters and peered into the depths, where they saw sea urchins and other sea creatures, enjoying themselves greatly. There were no fish to catch, despite Peter's notable efforts and Dieter's earnest suggestions.

But they also didn't see a shipwreck, or anything related, anywhere, despite the dives and underwater searches that went on for hours. The same thing happened the next day and the day following. They searched again in the places they had already tried, just to preclude the possibility that something had escaped them.

Meanwhile, Dieter was disturbed by the fact that he had

not had a chance to see Carla again, with Peter's absorption in the shipwreck saga adding to his displeasure. *After days, they had come up with nothing.* But, undeterred, Peter didn't want to go to visit Chora again or do anything else. His mind was focused entirely on the shipwreck. He looked at the maps, rechecked them, studied the depths, cleared his throat, scratched his head and started all over again. He was in a strange place with the issue, unlike anything Dieter had seen in the past.

"Well, what the hell has happened to get him into such a fury?" Dieter thought to himself. He wondered "how had this tall tale infected him so? How is it possible for him to suffer such an obsession? What if the shipwreck and its treasure don't exist? What will happen then? Will he go nuts?" Such thoughts ran through his mind. "At least I met Carla. Peter is going to drive *me* nuts with his obsession," he thought.

In the evenings, they ate at a taverna at the port and just took walks along the beach. They gathered some wood that the sea had washed up to the shore and Dieter painted what they found and made a mobile, hanging it in the window of their room. Dieter didn't want to go by himself to the village, but in reality, he thought about doing it. Naturally, he didn't want to abandon his friend, but Peter's obsession and egoism wore him out. Despite that, he decided to be patient for another day. "Hang on, Dieter, one more day. Peter will get bored and he'll want to make a jaunt to some other place. I'll bring it up today," he thought to himself.

That very evening, as they were again eating at the port, Dieter raised the issue, saying it would be nice if they went for a walk "even just for a drink at the village." Peter complained, noting that he wanted to get up early "to have the whole day ahead of him to continue the search with the dinghy since, when they found the treasure, it would take them days before they would raise it. So there wasn't any time to waste!"

"Anyway, Peter, we're just talking about having a drink!

We're not going to be up late. I promise!" Dieter said, trying to talk him into it. Peter finally agreed. So, paying the bill, they left the taverna and just managed to catch the bus. Arriving in the village, they decided to go to Andreas' bar "and maybe find the others", Dieter said. Peter didn't answer him.

At the bar, Andreas was sitting by himself. No one was there, since it was still early. Bob Dylan's famous song was playing. "Don't think twice. It's alright."

"Welcome, welcome! Come on in. You vanished. How are you doing?" said Andreas, greeting them.

"Hi Andreas? How are you? We stayed down at the port the last few days," they said apologetically in unison. "And the others? How are they doing?" Dieter asked with interest.

"All good. They might be coming by later. I talked earlier with Carla and Haris. Antonis might be coming too. Not sure. He had a date with his girlfriend."

"Great!" Dieter answered as Peter looked at him knowingly.

Not much time passed, in fact, before the figure of Carla appeared in the doorway. Behind her was Haris. They also sat at the bar and, after exchanging greetings, immediately started talking among themselves. Carla spoke almost continuously with Dieter, while Peter talked with Andreas and Haris about fishing and travel. In fact, all of them were well-traveled and experienced.

Haris invited the Germans and Carla and, of course, Andreas to come over to his place the following evening for a meal, stressing that he would make a fish soup-kakkavia, his specialty. "It's for our German friends, who have to try it!" Everyone happily accepted the invitation. Perhaps the happiest was Dieter. And beyond that, according to Haris' friends, he was an excellent cook. He had an enormous passion for food, especially the Greek cuisine and was a very hospitable, polite person, with humor and culture.

As a result, the invitation was something that Dieter looked forward to with impatient anticipation. He was already excited by the fact that he would see Carla again. Every time they met, he realized how much he liked her. He liked her character, her beauty, her tact, as they say, and generally her whole appearance. Perfect. He liked her more and more. As for her eyes, which had attracted him from the start, they were like to turquois pools the likes of which he had never seen. And they were also almond-shaped! As he thought about her, a smile broke out across his face.

Peter abruptly interrupted his musings. "What are you thinking about, Dieter? I see you're smiling. Maybe you are thinking about what you will do with the money we'll make from the treasure?"

"Well, not exactly, but almost," Dieter answered enigmatically. He didn't want to share his thoughts with his friend. It was a personal matter at this point and he was sure that Peter would not understand. Peter was totally focused on the treasure and the hunt to find it. *Everything else came second.*

In any case, Dieter thought, *he will eventually end up bitterly disappointed.* The thought comforted him. He didn't believe that, in fact, they would find a treasure at the bottom of the sea. "It's just sitting there waiting for us? And even if it does exist, *what then*?" he thought.

13

There are more things in heaven and earth, Horatio,

Then are dreamt of in your philosophy.

Hamlet

Shakespeare

P eter stubbornly persisted. How was it possible to find no signs of the shipwreck? They had already explored four coves, even its outer edges where it opened onto the sea, thinking maybe sea currents had caused the shipwreck to shift. But not a sign. "Nada. Nothing." Peter began to wonder if old man Timothy was telling him a tall tale under the influence of alcohol or maybe just made it all up. But that seemed unlikely. He didn't see him as a jokester. He seemed sincere, not a fabulist. Still, where in the devil was the terrible shipwreck? Maybe someone else had found it and taken it away? That couldn't, of course, be precluded. It was a possibility, and a serious one at that.

The situation was complicated, of course, because the

presumed location of the shipwreck was not somewhere you could anchor. Timothy had told him that and, indeed, insisted on it. Boats never went there for a swim. Only Timothy had dropped anchor there because the waters were so wonderful and his anchor happened to have a long chain. He was emphatic about that. Nor was the shipwreck in shallow waters. He himself, being young then, took a deep dive. "Then I had good lungs," he said. So where was the treasure? Maybe it only existed in Timothy's dreams? Who could be sure?

Peter hadn't mentioned any of this to Dieter because he was afraid of having a conversation where he would be told he was wrong to believe Timothy, and the like. In any case, Dieter had expressed his reservations, but didn't persist, seeing that Peter was so certain. So, poor Peter was in a stew because he couldn't externalize his doubts, anxieties and fears. Later, he tried to rationalize the whole situation, telling himself: *"Even if we don't find the treasure, we'll at least have a visit to the deep waters of Ios. Eagerly and with enthusiasm, we will see things of unique beauty."*

He glanced briefly into the sky. He saw some scattered clouds coming towards them. "I hope it's not going to rain," he thought. *That would ruin our search plans for the day.* Of course, it was still early morning. Just seven-thirty. He had woken up at daybreak. His friend was still sleeping like a baby and didn't hear anything. Motionless and quiet.

Peter prepared for himself an instant coffee and went out on the veranda, where he sat on a stone ledge. He had a number of ideas. Maybe they should have gone deeper, maybe the shipwreck had been dislodged and shifted further into the sea. So many years had passed and lots could have happened. The shifting of seabed plates, geological changes and other such phenomena. He was also concerned about this possibility. A lot in fact. He wasn't dumb. He knew the venture was difficult and uncertain. He had no illusions. Something inside him told him that the shipwreck was a genuine fact. It was somewhere to be found.

So where should they look? If the shipwreck had shifted, maybe it would be more difficult to extract the statues inside, once found, and that would mean that they maybe would need help from others. But who? And another dilemma he hadn't had time to figure out earlier. Where, in such a case, would they find help? Who could be trusted? "That's a big problem. Another thing that needed solving. And afterwards, how would they put the statues on offer? How would they sell them?"

All those issues now occupied his thoughts. He had put them aside because due to his excitement, leaving these technical issues unsolved. Of course, his orderly German thought-process would provide the answers. And fortunately, he wasn't the type to give up easily. He liked challenges. Up to now, he had been lucky with whatever he got involved with. Naturally, the other problems were nothing like his current venture. Not by a long shot. This caper was different than the other problems he had worked on. It wouldn't bring him down, as they say. Not at all. "He was a German. Strong and brave like Siegfried. Like the mythical hero of the Nibelungen," he thought to himself. He was certain, in fact, that he had gotten many things by right. That rigidity in his character was something that didn't sit well with some people. Not everyone liked him. He got along well with Dieter because they had been friends since childhood and a fraternal love connected them. In any case, Dieter had a milder disposition and was more loving. Dieter did not disturb or provoke him. Even when he objected to something, he would often let it pass. He avoided conflict and squabbling.

Peter knew this. Now, however, what would happen? Where in hell was the buried shipwreck? How long should they keep looking? Would it ever be found? And then there was the weather. When the winds started up, it wouldn't be feasible. He spent an hour thinking about it. Today, they would check out the next coves. He still had a shot. Starting tomorrow, the winds would be blowing, making it difficult to do the search with the dinghy. "Never mind. If we can't go searching, we'll take time to visit the island's beaches for some relaxing swims. We'll rent a car—it was already part of their plans. It'll make Dieter happy."

Today, however, he would make an enormous effort with the chance to search areas further to the north. Once the winds began that would not be easy. "And amid all this, Dieter found a love interest," he thought with a laugh. "Here we are trying to solve a problem and get rich and he found the time to fall in love. The fool! And he wouldn't listen to anything. Admittedly she was a beautiful woman, but she would drop him at some point. Are there no beautiful women in our country? Tall blonds with shapely bodies. The dummy found this Italian girl who has stunned him. We don't even know what she is like! For sure, she is always polite. She has manners and appears to be cultivated, and that's maybe why he liked her, poor fool.

Inside the room, Dieter could be heard getting up from bed and going to the bathroom.

"Where are you, Peter? Are you sitting outside?"

"Yes. Come on out and we'll have coffee. I didn't want to wake you. You were sleeping so well," he said laughingly.

The two friends sat out on the veranda under the shade of a tamarisk, a tree very common in the Cyclades.

"So? How do things look to you?" Peter said playfully.

"Let it be, Peter. I just woke up. I'm not in the mood for conversation. And first of all, please don't talk to me about the shipwreck."

"Understood. Drink your coffee first. In any case, I have good news for you."

"Oh, like what?" a surprised Dieter replied.

"Yes. I was thinking we should rent a car tomorrow and take some trips around the island. To see other places, other beaches. What do you say?"

"Yes. At last! You came to your senses. A bit late, but at last. Bravo. A good thought. Let's go to the other side to Magganari. It has a terrific beach and amazing water, Carla told me!"

"Her again, and you told me you wouldn't mention her name," Peter replied mockingly.

"Why, what's the matter? I also read about it on the Web. And, really, what's your problem? Don't tell me you are envious! Because you didn't find anyone. What a surprise! Your mind is so fixed on the shipwreck, which God only knows if it exists. Ha! You're a case for the books."

"Yes, so you say. It exists for sure. Timothy was certain. He wasn't joking. There is a huge treasure, ancient and unique. I'll find it even if the world perishes.

"May it be. I hope so too so. But let's also have some vacation time. Not just work!"

"OK, Dieter. It's all going to happen. Don't worry. You'll have your vacation. And if the Italian woman is part of that, I don't know. I wish you well if that's what you want."

"Since it is so early, Peter. I'm going to have for a second coffee. Do we have the coffee pods? Don't bug me. Carla, however, is a remarkable woman, and yes, I like her. Is that okay with you?"

He got up abruptly and went in to make another coffee, leaving Peter shaking his head.

After all that, Dieter made his second coffee while Peter decided to go down to the port in order to prepare the boat, fuel it, and take along some supplies like water and some sandwiches, since it looked like it would be a long day. Today, he planned to do some spear fishing, which he was good at, in contrast with Dieter, who wasn't. He was going to try to catch a large fish. Since they were going to dine with the others, if he caught something, he wanted it to be good. "No problem, maybe a white grouper perhaps. The grouper is cunning, but what a divine fish!" He had eaten that fish numerous times when he went on vacation with his parents back in the day. Unforgettable! Still, whatever he caught would be fine. "Since the best fish are the fresh ones. That's what they say and so it is."

Being a German, Peter was a perfectionist. The day was brilliant. The scattered clouds had disappeared and the water was smooth. It was waiting for them with anticipation. By the time Dieter showed up, the dinghy was ready to launch them on their adventure in the dream-like sea of Ios. Peter started up the engine. In a while they were in the open sea.

"Today I'm going for sure to catch a fish. I feel it," Peter said, adding "we're dining together today and I wanted to bring something."

"Yeah. That would be good. But if you don't catch anything, never mind. We can take the wine. Right?"

Peter turned out to be right. He caught a two-kilo whitefish but also a large sea bass, also weighing around two kilos or more. He also caught two octopuses. Very good sea creatures. He was excited, so much so in fact, that he didn't even complain about not finding any traces of the shipwreck. To be sure, they did an exhaustive search. They searched in the depths again and again, more or less in line with the coastline, but nothing. The shipwreck was nowhere to be found.

Around five o'clock, Peter signaled for the return. They got back to the port, tied up the craft and headed towards their room. After a shower, they sat on the veranda drinking coffee. They had put the fish in the refrigerator. They would pack it up to take with them to Haris' place just before leaving for the climb to Chora. Dieter was particularly happy. He would be able to see Carla again. For his part, Peter was proud of having caught all those fish. It was enough to feed everyone, plus seconds.

Around 8:15, they took the bus and went up to Chora. Haris' place was very close to the central square and they found it easily.

Andreas and Carla had already arrived and were drinking wine with Haris, who was in the middle of cooking. He was making *kakavia* (fish soup), as he had promised.

"Welcome! Come on over and take a seat at the table!" Haris said as he led them to his kitchen and eating area. The house was a charming traditional house, white inside with beautiful old furniture and lots of books. They went by the living room, which had two wooden island-style couches and two seemingly comfortable arm chairs. There also was a cupboard with crockery and a small table for the television. They were guided to the kitchen, which was two steps below the living room. The kitchen was spacious. It had a large table in the middle with two benches and a window that looked out beyond the village to the other side. It was a very charming house. Warm and simple, with island colors and a happy aura.

Peter gave Haris the fish and two octopuses. Haris, along with Andreas, explained that they were already cooking *kakavia*, so that the fish and octopus were, in fact, more than they could eat. So they agreed to grill one of the fish and keep the octopus and the other fish—the divine one—for the next day.

Haris was a good host. He offered to prepare the food his friends could eat the next day, when Antonis was sure to come. Everyone was cheerful and in a good mood, in particular Dieter, who kept his eyes on Carla as he ate. And she too seemed in a particularly good mood.

The *kakavia* was ready. The friends served themselves from the pot placed in the middle of the table. Also on the table was a tomato salad and bread, as well as white wine. Meanwhile, Haris had put the fish on the grill.

"Dear friends, welcome to my house! I wish you health and everything good. Whatever each of you wants!" Haris said, raising his glass as he made the toast.

The others did the same.

The soup was truly amazing. They enjoyed it greatly. Haris had really hit the spot with his soup. The fish was finally ready and was also excellent. Most of them ate without oil-and-lemon sauce, except for Peter, who added lemon only. The meal was in full swing, with wine in abundance. In full tilt, Haris started reciting his poems, which unfortunately the Germans couldn't understand. Andreas translated for them. Everyone cheerfully applauded the poet-cook!

Carla had started a chat with Dieter, whose intent listening suggested that they were talking about something important. Haris, Peter and Andreas started talking about fishing, octopuses and fishing grounds, since they were all experienced on such matters. The high spirits of the group were infectious.

Sometime after twelve o'clock, the group broke up, since Carla had to work at the hotel in the morning for her shift, she explained. They agreed to meet to dine the next day at Haris' again for another feast of fish. Calling a taxi, the Germans left with Carla. First they would take Carla to the hotel and then the two Germans would go back to the port.

Andreas had left a bit earlier to open his bar, late this time, but he had left a notice on the door outside.

It was indeed a very successful evening. Everyone left happy. Each for their own reason.

The night was magical. The moon was in hiding, allowing the stars to shine brightly.

Dieter was extremely enthusiastic, as he was sure he would see Carla again in a few hours. He didn't say a word about this to Peter, since he didn't want to hear his comments. He thought about her intensely until he fell into bed and was overtaken by sleep.

14

He was a very parfit gentle knight.

Canterbury Tales

Chaucer

Carla was skeptical. She had arrived at work by morning, but there wasn't much going on. It was already noon and, unlike other days, there wasn't anything to do. No arrivals were expected right now. Most likely, based on the reservations, there would be the next day.

She thought about Dieter. She couldn't understand what the younger of the two Germans saw in her and led him to chat with her the whole evening at yesterday's meal. Certainly, what he had to say was interesting and he had a talent for telling stories and a good sense of humor. He was handsome. She enjoyed being around him. But she couldn't understand why he paid so much attention to her. "Strange," she thought. He must be five or six years younger than she was. "Who knows?" That didn't seem to bother him. The truth was that their discussion

SAILING THE WATERS OF IOS

showed him to be unusually mature for his age. He must be around thirty-two, at most thirty-five, but he seemed young. He was a graphic artist, he said, but also played the flute. He also painted. He worked in a family antique shop in Hannover and had two siblings. But why did he tell her all these things?

For her part, she had said nothing about family matters, except that she had studied Fine Arts...nor had he asked any questions. Very strange! Maybe he just had the need to talk to someone. But then, why didn't he just talk with his friend? Of course, his friend would have known all about him, since they were childhood friends. And the other things he told her —how much he loved Italy and how much he wanted to live there sometime. He looked into her eyes knowingly. She couldn't make sense of it. But the way he stared left a great impression. He was more than friendly. Maybe he was attracted to her? No. Not possible. He was just being polite. In any case, sooner or later it would become clear if it was politeness or something else. But that was something she didn't even want to think about. *"Impossible. I can't imagine. And I'm not up for it right now. Put it out of your mind. He's just being polite."*

Her telephone rang, breaking into her thoughts. It was Haris. He wanted to suggest they get together again for food, like they said the night before, because they had to eat the other fish, which was terrific, as well as the octopus.

"That's fine. I'll come around 7:30 or 8. Is that good?"

"Yes. I wanted to ask if you wanted to come a little earlier so we could have time to chat and have a few laughs. It was great yesterday, no? Very nice guys. That's what I see every time we are together. What was Dieter talking to you about for so long? He focused on you a lot."

"We talked about different things. About his family business, about his interests and how much he liked Italy and so on."

"Ah yes. It seems he likes you."

"You think so? I doubt it. He's just being polite and maybe had the need to talk to someone. Who knows?"

"Maybe. Time will tell. He's good looking and polite, with good manners. More polite than Peter, who is somewhat aggressive, I thought. Dieter is kind.

"Yes...so he seems."

"I get the impression you like him."

"Maybe he feels friendlier because I am Italian. He's a cultured person, you see, and has inclinations towards painting and the fine arts. He told me his parents have an antique shop."

"Ah, yes. He got into details I see!"

"In any case. What can I say?"

"Don't bring anything for the meal. I've got everything, including dessert. I am going to make some baklava. I've got the ingredients."

"Good deal, Haris. See you this evening."

The phone call ended and Carla continued to think about the conversation. She entered some bills into the computer and then went to her room to relax. Time passed. She thought about what to wear that evening. She finally decided to wear jeans and a white blouse. That would be comfortable. She took a shower and then stretched out to sleep for an hour, enabling her body to rest. She wanted to be rested for the evening. But she didn't manage to sleep a wink.

Her mind was filled with thoughts that didn't let go. She was already forty years old (really, how had time passed so quickly?) and even though she liked children and wanted some of her own, she had not been lucky. Not because she was unable to, but because circumstances worked against her. She got pregnant when she was 19 during a brief relationship with a fellow student at the School of Fine Arts, but it didn't last. She decided not to have the child. How could she have a child when she herself was still a child? How would she take on the responsibility when it was with someone she was splitting from? Later, on another occasion, she got pregnant again, and again with the wrong person.

She was forced once more to go ahead with an abortion. She thought that, being very young, she had lots of time before her. But life was not kind to her. Family problems began with the death of her father and the economic problems that followed. Then there was her mother's illness and the trouble with her crazy sister. She had lots of burdens to bear. Did she have regrets about the abortions? Yes. And in both cases. She should have been bolder, even if it meant raising them on her own. She was overcome by "reason". Now, at forty, it was nearly impossible. Nor was she in a relationship. She had broken up recently with Andy, though he by no means would have been the right person. Anyway. In fact, if she had been more courageous, she would have done something. But she never took the chance. With her present state of mind, she would have. *But now, as the saying goes, the bird has flown the coup.*

15

The beautiful is always strange.

Charles Baudelaire

P eter arranged to rent a car for a few days, for as long as the weather stayed windy. He found a small, gold-colored Suzuki Jimny jeep, which was just right for their holidays and their excursions. On their agenda were dirt roads, but they also intended to check out from the shore places where the shipwreck might have taken place. It would give them another perspective. With that in mind, they had brought along from Germany some binoculars.

He also, however, was thinking about Dieter, who would be elated by the car rental, since he was fed up with of all the days of searching. It would enable Peter to escape Dieter's complaining. They also would be going to different places with beautiful beaches, of which the island had many. After all, it was a holiday! He didn't want to give away the fact that he was looking for something in particular!

They went back to the shop to return the diving equipment since they would not be needing them for a few days. They would rent them again when they starting searching the depths again.

He returned to the room to find Dieter talking on the telephone with his sister. Everything is OK at home, his sister told him. They were missed, but they hoped he was having a good time in Greece. "I don't imagine you'll be having arguments with Peter," his sister asked, but was immediately reassured by Dieter. "Everything is just fine. It's a beautiful island. You have to come sometime. You'll like it. It's magical. The sea is something else. Better than anything we've seen before."

After the phone call and drinking of coffee, the two friends put on their swim suits, grabbed their beach towels, swim fins and masks, got in the car and headed for some beaches. First they would go to Mylopotas and then head toward Kolitsani, which Peter had learned from Andreas was very beautiful. That evening, they had an invitation from Haris for fish. Their program for the day was full.

The sea at Mylopotas was beyond anything you could imagine. Fantastic in every sense of the word. It was among the most beautiful beaches in existence, not just in Greece, but in the world. That's the conclusion the two friends reached, in total agreement without the slightest hesitation.

The two Germans did a lot of swimming using fins and masks. They gazed at the amazing bottom with its sea creatures, and after an hour they came out and sat on the sand. They were warmed by the sun's rays. The sun's warm caress was just what was called for after the cool waters of the sea.

Dieter was in high spirits, but had another reason for being so: In a few hours, he would see Carla again. He was already fantasizing about their next encounter. A welter of questions occupied his thoughts. "So what did she think? She seemed happy every time she saw him. Still, she hadn't shown anything more specific on the issue at hand. Did she like him or not?"

Peter interrupted his thoughts abruptly, suggesting that they go to the beach bar for a drink. "A chilled beer would be perfect right now. What do you think?" Sitting in the shade under a thatched umbrella, they enjoyed their cold beers and looked out at the sea that was glimmering in the sunlight.

Later, they went for another dip to Kolitsani, which had a smaller, relatively quiet beach and was not far away. What wonderful water! So clear and clean, Spectacular!

At 6 o'clock, they returned to the port. It was still hot. They sat on the veranda of their studio and ate some peaches they had chilled in the refrigerator. The magical view of the sea and a sense of satisfaction overcame them. "It's beautiful here, no Dieter?" Peter said, being in a good mood at that moment. Later, they washed off the sea-salt and laid down. Dinner at Haris' was for 8 o'clock. They didn't have to do any shopping, since they had already brought the fish and octopus. They felt very positive about the get together and the food that would be part of it. These were mainly Peter's thoughts, since Dieter had other things on his mind that had nothing to do with food.

They would go by car, so they wouldn't be dependent on the bus schedule. Everything was under control, at least for the moment.

16

But if I'm content with a little,
Enough is as good as a feast.

Love in a Village

Isaac Bickerstaffe

Loumir had been working for three years at the shop that rented diving equipment. His boss was a good person and paid him on time. He had no complaints. He had left his family in a village in Albania and had come to Greece to find a job. His father was a farmer, but a physical disability had downed him in recent years, leaving him unable to work. His brother, sister and mother tended the fields.

Loumir decided to take off on his own. He was strongly built and work didn't bother him. It was enough that he got paid. He sent back as much money as he could to Albania. He first work was in Piraeus in a metal working shop, but then he found his current job from a fellow Albanian who, returning to his country, recommended him.

Loumir wanted to make money, lots of money, so that he could then return to his homeland. He searched for an opportunity and kept his eyes open. In truth, he had few reservations about how. He did not feel sympathy for others, since he believed that life had treated him unjustly. He had no room to be sensitive, as he saw it. He was agile and clever. He knew how to maneuver and how to adapt like a chameleon. He observed those around him and was polite in order to make a good impression and gain their trust. He aimed to learn who had money and how he could benefit. And in what way.

So, he took note of how easy Peter had been about renting the diving equipment. He didn't bargain over the prices. He didn't offer any information about where he was planning to dive or ask any questions about where the best places were to do so. As if he was indifferent to the matter. He held on to the equipment for many days and said that he would need them again. Somehow something didn't fit together for Loumir, or Loumi, as he boss called him. He had the feeling that something peculiar was going on with the German. He had the impression that he wasn't interested in diving for sport. So what was it?

He intended to talk to a friend of his, also an Albanian, Emver, who worked at a restaurant on the port. For sure, Emver had no idea about the sea, nor did he know how to swim very well, nor did he have any experience with these kinds of matters, but Loumir needed some extra help, an extra pair of hands and eyes. "That German, and his tall blonde friend are up to something," he thought. He felt instinctively that something suspicious was going on. The Germans had not rented the equipment just to check out sea creatures in the deep. Tracking their movements seemed worth the effort.

17

Life is a jest, and all things show it.

I thought so once, but now I know it.

My Own Epitaph

John Gay

At 8:10, the two Germans rang Haris' doorbell. Carla opened the door for them, since Haris was already in the kitchen. He was cooking the octopus which, as Dieter soon determined, smelled wonderful. At the same time, Haris had lit the fire to grill the fish, while boiling the potatoes everyone liked. He would put parsley on them, he told Peter, who had hurried to the kitchen, led by his nose.

"It smells perfect! How are you cooking the octopus?" Peter asked with curiosity. "The aroma is exquisite!"

"It's very easy. I boil them in their own juices, that is, without water, on a low heat. If I am at the sea, I add three spoons of sea water. If not near the sea, I make a sauce by adding a little vinegar and maybe some oil when it is close to done cooking. That's a sea recipe. That's how we used to make it when I was young and we plied the seas of the Aegean in boats years ago. We also did sail-boating back then," he said with a hint of melancholy.

"Great. They smell amazing. Let me have a taste! Don't forget, I have an interest in food. We have eating places in Hannover. So they will be interested in new tastes and recipes! I hope you'll give it to me later in detail."

"I hope you like it. I'm certain you will be pleased. And of course, I'll give it to you. And it should be a smash hit in Hannover!"

"And the fish. How do you cook it?"

"I cut it into slices and grill it in the oven. You can eat it with olive oil and lemon and, of course, with parsley or without, or even without olive oil. Just a little lemon and salt and pepper. Depends on your taste. Of course, it also goes with mayonnaise, but I don't like it on fresh fish. In any case, it has its own flavor and it's fresh, so my preference is to eat it plain with just a little pepper."

"Perfect! I'll try it that way. It's a wonderful fish, and since I caught it, I'm sure I'll like it."

In the living room, Carla was talking with Dieter about the island's beautiful beaches and, responding to his questions, told him the story of how she ended up staying permanently on Ios.

"The truth is that I was enchanted by the island... its beaches, its nature, its villages. Everything together, the atmosphere. I wouldn't want to live anywhere else. Then I found work and made enough money to live in this amazing place. Understand?" Dieter nodded affirmatively. "Yes, I totally understand." He too was enchanted with the island, but also with her, he thought to himself slyly, looking intensely into her eyes. Deep within her eyes, he saw her truth—a truth she herself was unaware of. He felt her with all his being.

The doorbell rang and Carla ran to answer. It was Andreas and almost immediately appearing behind him was Antonis with his girlfriend.

"Welcome! Is everything OK?", Carla asked opening the door. Cheerfully Andreas entered holding a bottle of white wine.

The meal was exquisite. They ate royally, as Antonis, who was very particular, put it. Their conversation covered a lot of topics: their experiences, politics, the damage tourism had done to the Cycladic islands, "but which, on the other hand, is essential for keeping the islands populated, for the youth as well, providing jobs". But they also discussed a lot of other things, among them about ancient Homer, who had been a native of Ios. Finding the opportunity, Haris began reciting his poems, as he often did:

Five chaps

But also five shooting stars

Made me stay here,

Forever,

Beautiful island,

Beloved daughter of the sea

He recited the poem with feeling. "It's one of my older ones!" he stressed. The group applauded and he recited more. Carla suddenly realized that Dieter was staring at her persistently. She returned the look. *Their relationship seemed to be taking an interesting turn.* And so the evening unfolded.

18

Lift up your heart.

Sursum Corda

The day after the meal at Haris' place, Dieter went up to Chora early in the morning. Peter was still sleeping and he didn't want to wake him up. He purposely avoided that because he didn't want to tell him exactly what he planned to do in the village, what his purpose was. And not, of course, to hear his criticism or for his friend to disrupt his plans.

He went by Antonis' shop and, without hesitating, asked him for Carla's phone number. Antonis gave it to him without asking questions. In any case, the situation had become obvious. Everyone had more or less recognized his interest, as well as the sympathy towards him shown by Carla. They also wanted to see her happy after all that she had gone through. They loved her and she was their friend. They didn't want to interfere with something that could possibly make her happy. For sure, Dieter's company had distracted her from her problems. Everyone understood that.

So everything was fine. Beyond that, it was a matter of her deciding how far she wanted their relationship to go. After all, she was a grown up! She had judgment, taste and standards!

As soon as he got her phone number, Dieter almost flew out of Antonis' shop and called her on his mobile phone. At first, Carla was startled by his call. The hesitancy in her voice was apparent. Dieter stuttered at first and almost lost it, but regained his composure. "I'd like to get together for a coffee," he said. "I've got a lot of things I want to ask you about and I need your advice."

In reality, he didn't have anything specific to ask her, but he had to say something to justify meeting her in private. Meanwhile, he thought about what he would say to her. Something that would stick. He didn't want to appear foolish. It was a delicate balance.

They finally met at the square for one of its famous coffee houses. It was obvious that words were not needed at this point. Nevertheless, Dieter made an earnest effort to show that he really did want to ask her something. What would that be? To help him find a small, reasonably-priced house to buy.

"I like this island and I want to come here often, in addition to my summer holidays," he told her. "I'd prefer to have my own place, even if it's small. I don't want to spend a lot of money. But since, as you told me, you too are looking for something, I thought I would ask you to let me know if you see something maybe appropriate you aren't interested in. I can fix it up and make it right for a vacation stay. I could also bring along some family, if they wanted to come."

His justification for meeting was clearly weak, but Carla pretended to go along. She didn't ask him many details, or whether he had also asked Andreas or Antonis. So they exchanged phone numbers and discussed prices and possible locations. At some point, Dieter took her hand and held it for a long time. She looked at him with a questioning gaze, but she didn't draw it back. Then Dieter, overcoming his natural shyness, tilted his head towards her and kissed her on the mouth. The kiss was soft and sweet and Carla responded without thinking about where the situation was heading. It seemed so natural to her that she made no effort at avoidance. He had caught her unprepared.

"I've got to get going," she told him. "I've left work in the middle of things." Dieter paid and they got up to leave. "Great. I'll see you this evening," he said firmly, in a manner that broached no objection. He himself was surprised by his boldness.

"OK. This evening!" she told him. She looked into his eyes smilingly. Without thinking, he embraced her in a quick motion, pulling her towards him. And she surrendered. She didn't put up any resistance. After the surprise, he stroked her hair and so they separated. Carla was stunned by the whole scene, and he found himself in emotionally dazed, floating on a cloud. Overjoyed.

Dieter head towards Antonis' shop like mechanically to buy some tea and some other minor items, but mainly to recover emotionally from the meeting. It was as if he had been in a head-on automobile collision. He would see Carla again that evening, he thought.

That same evening, though, unluckily for him, Carla called and told him, somewhat coldly, that she wouldn't be going out that evening "because she was tired."

"Alright, as you say," he responded, feeling deflated, but adding hastily, "We'll talk again tomorrow."

"OK", she answered without emotion and ended the call.

He was startled. He was disappointed, greatly in fact, since he desired to see her, but he did not insist. He couldn't insist. He realized that things had moved quickly, especially for a woman like Carla. He respected her hesitancy. But he was certain now that she wanted him as well. That was what mattered. For sure, she liked him. "Otherwise, why bother with me at all," he thought.

As for Carla, her mind was in a blur. She didn't know where this was leading. She hadn't judged him correctly. She wanted his company. She liked him. She liked that he liked her. She needed the presence of a man in her life that was more than just a friendship. She liked the fact that this young, attractive man had flirted with her. That was one thing. Another was what happened when they met for coffee. She hadn't yet processed it. It had developed so quickly. She hadn't expected such a serious situation to develop, and so abruptly.

"Never mind. I'll see how I feel and think about it in those terms. I didn't sign anything in blood. We're just talking about a kiss and mutual sympathy after all!" she thought. And then began to see other dimensions. "Forget about the fact that he is younger than me. That didn't seem to bother him at all!" she thought to herself. But it did matter to her. The whole thing is pretty risky. He was very handsome. And as for herself? She wasn't in the first bloom of youth. Once, indeed, she was very beautiful. But now? "But really. It's not a monumental event. It was a sudden kiss. That doesn't mean a relationship, for heaven's sake!"

Despite all this sober reasoning, she was shaken. She felt like she had received a blow to her stomach. Her heart was fluttering. She was in a state of nervous anxiety which, rather than abating, grew more intense with every passing hour. Unable to calm down, she lay down on her bed and took a mild tranquilizer that finally enabled her to doze off still thinking of the tall, gentlemanly German, with the characteristically interesting haircut.

For his part, Dieter was equally upset and feeling blue. He wasn't interested in going to Chora or to mix with the group. He didn't say a word to Peter about what had happened with Carla.

He kept it to himself. He didn't want to share anything. He didn't want to hear Peter's opinion or criticism or comments. He told him that he had a headache and went to curl up in his small bed. He didn't eat dinner and pretended that he was sleeping so he could avoid talking to his friend. In short, he was closed within himself and his thoughts.

He desired Carla enormously. It wasn't just a passing fancy. He wasn't that kind of person. He was, in fact, very choosey. He wasn't indiscriminate in his taste for women. German women seemed vacuous to him. Nor did he lower his standards for what he wanted from a woman just in order not to feel lonely. He couldn't care less. He wanted her and her alone. She was unique and he liked her a lot. She had something special, he thought, which had struck a chord within him. He felt that there was a mystery surrounding her personality. There was an atmosphere, an indefinable feeling when he was around her, which he felt but he couldn't yet explain or express clearly. Within him, he also was certain that she felt something for him too.

"She must want me, since she responded to my touch and kiss. And when I held her to me, she relaxed in my arms. She wants me. I feel it. I'm sure I'm not mistaken!" he mused, as his thoughts swirled continuously in his head.

Peter was observing his friend out of the corner of his eyes, but he didn't dare bother him with questions and talk. He respected the fact that his friend was not feeling well.

19

I arise from dreams of thee
in the first sleep of night,
When the winds are breathing low,
And the stars are shining bright

Lines to an Indian Air
Shelley

T he day was glorious. Dieter woke up in the morning and drank a black coffee standing up. He had decided to go to the mini-mart to shop for a few breakfast items, but also different cheeses and deli foods that would be handy for a quick meal. They were also out of coffee.

He had just gotten into the market when he heard a voice shouting at him: "Dieter! Is it you? What are you doing here, my friend?" Turning around, he saw his old friend Otto from Hannover, who he had regularly played music with. "Otto! What are you doing here? I'm with a friend of mine and we're on holiday! We've been on this fantastic island for several days. And you?"

I'm here with four friends. Maybe you know one of them. We have a fifty-three-foot boat that we rented for our vacation.

We just got here yesterday, but we've already done a number of islands. Do I know your friend?"

"No, I don't think so. He's an old family friend. His name is Peter."

"Great! We can get together. Why don't you come down to the boat now and we can have some coffee? You can meet the others."

Dieter nodded affirmatively. "So fine. Why not? Let's go. Are you sure you want company so early in the morning?"

"Sure! I wouldn't have said so otherwise," Otto said emphatically.

Finishing their shopping and paying, the two young men headed towards Otto's boat. It was a large yacht, a Beneteau sailing boat. French. Very spacious, contemporary and beautifully designed.

"What a great boat, Otto! It's huge," Dieter said in awe.

"Yes. It's fabulous. It has a lot of innovations and the design is very modern. We paid plenty, but it was worth it!" Otto said, then calling his friends to come up and help with the groceries.

"Walter, Helmut! Come on up and help. We have a guest."

From inside the boat two blonde giants emerged. They were Otto's friends. One of them, Walter, was blonde with blue eyes and long hair down to his shoulders, laughing and cheerful. The other, Helmut, was a curly-haired blonde, shirtless in orange bermudas. Both were athletically fit.

"This is Dieter. We're friends from Hannover and play music together once a week or so. Dieter plays the flute!"

"Really?" Walter said. "Just imagine finding each other here. What a coincidence!"

After making introductions, the four went down into the boat for a leisurely chat and drank coffee. Otto's other two friends were still sleeping: Max from Berlin and Johann, an old schoolmate of Walter, and Otto also from Hannover.

They talked about the islands and their various trips to Greece and elsewhere, since they all were travelling types. A while later, Max and Johann woke up, after introductions, they had coffee and fruit Walter prepared. At some point, Helmut rolled a cigarette with "a very fine, special weed", he noted.

He offered it to the others and to Dieter, who was generally not a participant, but so as not to ruin the companionship also took a few tokes, even though he wasn't a cigarette smoker. It made him dizzy and the world began to spin around. For a moment, he thought he had lost it and had a brief illusion. But he managed to get it together after first drinking some water and downing two or three biscuits. The conversation continued with jokes, stories and lots of laughter.

The laughter was cut short when Dieter's phone rang. It was Peter. "I'll be back in five minutes," he said.

"Come back with your friend for coffee," Otto told Dieter as he was leaving.

"Fine. I'll give you a call. We're close by. We'll drop by for sure. He also is interested in boats. Thanks to you all. It was a pleasure!"

20

The Uncertainty Principle isis is the principle of the indeterminate.

Werner Heisenberg

1927

*T*he noise was terrifying. A muffled roar, unearthly, shaking everything living. The roar was so violent that it froze the blood of anyone there at that moment.

For a second, Dieter lost his balance. He was traumatized when he saw things swaying back and forth and the whole building shaking. He was again at Antonis' store buying herbs and tea when the whole structure began to shake, as if a giant had seized it and swayed it back and forth.

"Earthquake, earthquake!" Antonis shouted and directed him to get out fast, pulling him out of his shop, which was shifting around like a cardboard box.

"Whoa...what the devil is that, an earthquake?" a traumatized Dieter said. He had stopped in his tracks. It was in fact an earthquake, he realized, and a strong one. Dieter had never lived through anything like that. Scary. He never had that kind of experience and, naturally, he lost it.

"We'll see on the news where the epicenter was. It's a strong one, I think," Antonis said. They both stayed outside on the road for a long time recovering from the shock. Antonis explained to Dieter that in Greece, earthquakes were not rare. To the contrary.

A passerby, also distressed by the sudden happening, informed that it had been a 5.5 Richter quake, which is to say, pretty strong, but fortunately with an epicenter, he explained, somewhere in the sea between the Cyclades and Crete, resulting in there being no severe damage. Nor were there been any mention of deaths. "Just as well," he told them, also shaken. "There's nothing worse than an earthquake."

Dieter immediately called Peter to check in on him. His friend was in their room at the port sleeping. When he realized what was happening, he ran out to the terrace. Carla called immediately after. First to Dieter, who was surprised, and then asking for Antonis and talking to him for a while. She seemed to be calmer than the others, saying that it was pretty routine, due to the fact that Italy was also an earthquake prone country and she was used to small quakes. But everyone was shaken, some more than others. More than anything, it was the noise that frightened. It told them that they were totally vulnerable and weak in face of the roaring earth. They agreed to meet that evening to have a beer and a bite to eat at the village square.

Naturally, the topic of discussion everywhere was the earthquake. Everyone, young and old, locals and foreigners, talked about it. The patrons at the coffeehouse, passers-by, Antonis' customers. Everyone on the island. The event had frightened and shaken them to the point that some of them said they planned to spend the night outside their homes.

◆ ◆ ◆

After recovering from the shock, Dieter began his trek down the steps to the port. Halfway there, he stopped to catch his breath and call Carla. The telephone rang twice and Carla answered: "Hey Dieter. Are you OK?"

"Yeah. I was headed down to the port and wanted to hear your voice. How are you? Were you frightened? I was worried about you, Carla."

"Naturally I was frightened, but I'm familiar with earthquakes. But how are you?"

"Look, it was distressing. I've never experienced anything like that. But now it's passed and, fortunately, the quake happened in the sea, someone told us."

"Yes. I heard that on the news."

"Are we going to meet, Carla? Would you like to? I want to see you. If you want, I can come now. I'll turn around and come up to see you."

"Now? Well, maybe. Do you really want to come back up? What to say? Do you really want to come? I still have some work to do."

"OK. It's not a problem. I'd like to see you. I'll come by and wait until you're finished. I'm coming," Dieter said firmly.

"Good. Come on. But we won't stay here long. I want to go up and get some rest."

"OK. I'll be there soon."

Overjoyed, he turned around and started to leap up the steps. It was hard to restrain himself. "Why did I tell her I wanted to see her? How insistent I was. Good for me," he thought. Then, to avoid questions, he sent an SMS to Peter saying that he was staying in the village and would be late, so "don't wait for me if you want to go for a swim." He didn't want to get involved in a discussion. In twenty minutes, he reached Carla's hotel. She was at the reception desk arranging room reservations for some English guests.

Dieter settled into a couch near the door and waited patiently. Finishing with the guests, Carla came over to him. "So you came!"

"Yes. I wanted to see you."

"Fine, then. What should we do? Are you hungry? Should we eat something, or would you rather just have a coffee?"

"I'd like to be somewhere private, so to speak, so we can chill. If we can, we can eat a snack. A sandwich would be OK for me. And a beer. Can we maybe go to your room to hang out?"

"My room isn't too large, you know."

"Doesn't matter to me, Carla. It's just a matter of having some peace-and-quiet."

Fine. So let's get some sandwiches and beer and go on up."

"Sounds good," Dieter said, not concealing his enthusiasm.

They went to the bar, each ordering a sandwich and a beer, as well as bottles of water. They headed towards Carla's room.

The room was pleasant, with white walls and lots of light, blue curtains and a small couch next to the double bed. There also was a flat screen TV. The view from the window was marvelous, since you could see the glittering sea. There was a balcony with two chairs and a metal table.

"Great room! It's not so small. Just fine," Dieter said.

"Yes. Well, it's good for the time being, until a find my own place."

"Where should we sit and eat? Outside? We can look out at the sea."

"Sure."

They sat on the balcony and ate their tasty sandwiches

and chilled beer.

"I like you, Carla," Peter said, turning around and taking her hand.

"Maybe you're being hasty? You don't know me at all," she answered hesitantly and with genuine surprise. No one in her life had ever made such a declaration to her so directly and quickly. *Dieter had caught her off guard.*

"But still, I feel like I know you. Something inside tells me that we are compatible."

"Really, do you think so?"

"Let's go inside, Carla. It's hot," Dieter said emphatically, with a decisiveness he wasn't generally known for. Going inside, Dieter laid on the comfortable bed and turned on the television. He started zapping to find a movie. Carla had gone to the bathroom to wash her hands.

"Come on out," Dieter said. "I found a movie to watch. Come sit next to me!"

The movie was *Body of Lies* with Russell Crowe and Leonardo di Caprio. Carla sat next to him. Without missing a beat, he embraced her and pulled her close. They sat embracing for some time until Dieter took her head in both hands and kissed her. It was a magic kiss, a kiss that betrayed their true feelings. They couldn't separate. Before the film was finished, Dieter had deftly undressed her, kissing her all over. She was still, enjoying his sweetness. Dieter liked her even more after seeing her shapely body. Carla drove him wild.

She then opened his shirt and unbuttoned his pants. They dived under the sheets and remained entwined until night fell. At some point, their nirvana was suddenly disrupted by the ring of Dieter's mobile phone. Naturally, it was Peter, so Dieter didn't answer. He would call him later after first finding a good excuse to avoid him. He decided, first of all, to send him an SMS. The message was that he was busy looking in Chora for something and would explain later. "I'll be back, but I'm not yet sure when", he wrote and urged him not to wait but to get something to eat if he was hungry.

Peter sent him a reply immediate, demanding to learn what the issue was, but the message remained unanswered. Meanwhile, Carla had gotten up and was observing the situation. "Dieter, was it Peter again? What are you going to tell him? I'd rather you didn't go into details."

"Of course not. Don't worry. I don't have any reason to mention anything. I'll tell him that at some moment we accidently ran into each other and that we went to see some houses."

"Hmmm. Do you think he'll believe you? Since you're close friends. It seems a bit weak."

"So what if he doesn't believe it. I'm not about to tell him anything. I'm not interested in hearing his opinion. Anyway, it's no concern of his. OK, at some point he will learn. I'll let him know. But not yet. We'll see when. Sometime. There's no rush. He knows that I'm attracted to you, but only that."

"Hahaha, you amaze me!" said Carla laughingly.

"I like you Carla and I'm not about to share right now what I feel with anyone except you, my sweet. Don't think I'm going to tell him everything. There are things he doesn't know about me."

"Fine. Come on then!" Another round of kisses followed. Their union was complete and unforgettable, both for Dieter and for Carla. More time passed until Carla said, "Should we get up? Are you hungry? Do you want to do something, maybe take a walk?"

"No. I don't want to go anywhere. We're just fine here. It's perfect. I want to hold you in my arms and enjoy being with you. Let's see a movie and chat. Unless maybe you've gotten bored with me."

"Of course not. Things are going beautifully. So let's see a movie. And what about food? Maybe we should order something. I'll call the kitchen. Is there something in particular you want to eat? What say you? They have really good beef filet with potatoes, if you're interested, and macaroni with sauce. What do you prefer?"

"Sounds good. Let's have meat. It will give us energy. Beef fillet and salad."

"Agreed. Beer or wine?"

"I'd prefer wine, if you do too. Whatever you want, my love."

"OK. I'm going to order. Beef fillet, salad and white wine. Red is too heavy...and two Coca Colas and water. Agreed?"

"Yes, my sweet. And it's on me. No objections!"

"No need. We are at the hotel."

"No. I insist. I'll pay this time. Your turn next time."

"Alright then."

Carla made the order and then went in the bathroom to take a shower. Dieter followed her in, washing her with warm water, like a precious doll.

"Good God. You're so beautiful!" he said. He relished looking her as she dressed, as did she as he dressed. What a wonderful body, strong and ripped, but slim, with fine limbs, a dreamy face. She realized that she had fallen in love with him. *Just like that. Hopelessly.* He was very good looking, and the funny thing was he didn't seem aware of it. He had a childlike, innocent manner, but at the same time, an unexpected maturity. A powerful combination. Very interesting and attractive, Carla thought.

They watched some television, the world news, and then did some zapping to find a movie to watch. They found a comedy, the charming "Blume in Love". An old film from the 1970s, but excellent, with George Segal, Susan Anspach and Chris Christofferson. They both laughed their hearts out. Meanwhile, the food arrived. Dieter paid the bill and they went out again on the balcony to eat. It was magnificent. All around the lights had gone on and a very romantic scene spread before them. Beyond was the sea. A ship was passing by far away and you could see its lights in the distance.

"How great it is, my sweet Carla! Unbelievable! Thank you!" he said.

"Yes, beautiful", she answered and smiled. "You know what? You make me very happy."

"You too."

"Excellent! We should celebrate. Let's drink to it."

They clink their wineglasses and Dieter declared theatrically: "To the most beautiful woman I have ever seen, who made me fall immediately in love!"

"Thanks, my sweet love. I'm so delighted we met!"

"Tell me about yourself. I want to know everything," he said.

"We have time for that. But tell me. I imagine you aren't in a relationship right now. Am I right?"

"No, nothing at all. Two years ago, I split with a woman I was going out with. Since then, nothing. I'm not the easiest person, you know."

"Hmm. I think you're just fine."

"Well OK, but I do have my quirks, you'll see. You'll get to know me little by little."

"Well, don't scare me off!"

"I'm telling you so you'll be ready!"

"You're sweet and I like you. That doesn't bother me. We all have our quirks."

"And you, beautiful. What are you hiding?"

"Nothing of great importance. I've had some problems. But let that be for now."

After the meal, they went into the room and continued watching the film.

"Tomorrow, what will we do? What do you say?" Dieter asked. "What time do you start work? In the morning again? Do you want to meet here again? Or no? Maybe you'd rather go out for a walk?"

"I work in the morning again. The others, all of them, will be looking for us. But if you want to meet here, that's fine with me. Really, I'd rather it be just the two of us."

"OK, later today I am going down to find Peter, who will be in a fury. But I'll come by tomorrow midday, early in the afternoon. What do you say? Maybe we can take a swim together. Agreed?"

"For sure. That would be great. But have you figured out what you are going to tell Peter?"

"Yes, I have. I'll tell him about the house, that we were doing the search together. Since I also want to find something to buy. Something like that. I'll tell him the next day. Of course, at some point, we'll have to get together with the others. But we still have time. What do you say?"

"I say, yes!"

They relaxed in an embrace, caressing each other as they nodded off. Carla woke up at some point with the impression that there had been an earthquake aftershock. A minor one, however.

"Dieter! Wake up, sweetheart! I think we had an aftershock. Did you feel it?"

"No my love. I didn't notice anything," he said puzzled.

"Are you going down to the port or not?"

"Yeah. I'm going. Can you call a taxi for me? Ah, what a nuisance. I'd like to stay. You're not worried, are you?"

"No. I'm fine. There are always little aftershocks. I'll make the call. Get dressed. They'll be coming pretty soon."

Dieter got up and brushed a comb through his hair. They left the room and walked in an embrace to the exit of the hotel. The taxi came quickly. Dieter kissed Carla, saying: "Bye my love. Tomorrow! I'll call you as soon as I can."

"Goodnight! I'll wait for your call."

21

Ask me no questions and I'll tell you no fibs.

She Stoops to Consquer

Oliver Goldsmith

The hour was late. Dieter arrived at the port, emerged from the taxi and headed by foot to the studio apartment. He called Carla to say goodnight and, now relaxed, walked quietly. The room was dark. Peter had gone to bed and was snoring.

Dieter moved cautiously so as not to wake him and, exhausted, he too fell into his bed. But his thoughts kept him from falling asleep right away. He was happy. He saw Carla's image in his head and thought about how sweet she was. At some point, filled with feelings for Carla, beautiful Carla, he finally fell asleep.

In the morning, Peter was the first to get up and make coffee. Dieter was still asleep. But the clatter woke him up. Unable to get back to sleep, he opened his eyes. Across from him he saw Peter with a puzzled look on his face.

"Good day, Dieter! Where were you last night, my friend? You were nowhere to be found," Peter said pompously.

"Hey, it's too early for this. I'm still waking up," said Dieter. But he could not escape the Peter's curiosity. As soon as he got out of bed, his friend started with the inquisition:

"So are you going to tell me at last where you were yesterday? I waited up late for you," he said with some resentment in his voice.

"Well, I met with Antonis and then, by chance, Carla. The earthquake happened, then later I went to see some houses with Carla, who is looking for a place to buy. But I also looked for myself. I'm interested in something small."

"Hmmm. The two of you? How so? And the house, what's that about? *Something new?*"

"I ran into her by accident. As for looking at houses, I thought about it and it seemed like a nice idea."

"But you spent so many hours looking at houses? Are you pulling my leg Dieter?"

"We sat and ate afterwards and passed the time talking."

"I see. The two of you?"

"Yes."

"And?"

"And what?"

"Did you make any progress? Did you learn anything about her? What kind of person is she? What did you talk about?"

"Lots of different things, mainly about the houses we had seen."

"Nothing else?"

"No, not really. Like what?"

"And so you also saw houses for yourself too? Anything of interest?"

"Some small places, but they need work, some a lot and others a little."

"Hmmm."

"In any case, I'm also going to look at a few more today. A real estate broker might come too. So if you'd like, we could take an early swim. Let's take the car so we aren't late getting back. Like I said, I want to go to Chora again and see more houses."

"And with Carla, of course, eh?"

"Yeah. So what's your problem? We're on holiday. I'd like to relax and have a good time too," Dieter said, annoyed.

"No, I was saying…"

"Fine. I don't have anything more to tell you, since there's nothing to say. So let's get ready to go."

They had a second coffee then got ready to leave the room. They went to a small beach just beyond Koumbara, where they had done some searching on previous days. Peter put on the swim fins and mask and dived into the deep. He swam quite a lot, but found nothing of interest. As for Dieter, he also took a dip, but without enthusiasm, getting out of the water soon to dry off in the sun.

Of course, he had some guilty feelings about leaving Peter alone again. So he thought that, when they got back, they could look for Otto and the guys and leave Peter with the group while he went to see Carla. "That's what I'll do! Lucky for me that the group of friends is here." That was a lifesaver. In any case, Otto's sailing companions were civil and fun. Peter would have a good time with them. What better company for his friend at the moment. Excellent. Good thing he had cut Peter off and came up with the idea, he thought, laughing to himself.

Fortunately for him, things worked out as planned. His

friends, the sailors with their ship, were at the port. They had just tied up the yacht. They greeted them heartily and, after having a coffee on board, Peter kept them company, while Dieter got up to leave and head for the village. But they all agreed to meet the next day and take the boat out to go for a swim.

Relieved that he had a fantastic idea, found good company for Peter to hang out with, Dieter was cheerful. Feeling lighthearted, free of obligations and without feelings of guilt, Dieter left the Germans and their yacht and went to get the automobile to drive to the village. In a hurry, he couldn't wait.

22

O happy race of men, if love,

which rules Heaven, rule our minds.

Consolations of
Philosophy

Boethius

He was longing to see Carla. His heart raced and chest fluttered. He was beginning to fall deeply in love. Soon, he headed towards the hotel where his beloved was. But ahead of time he called her to let her know in case it was awkward for her and she didn't want to meet him there.

"Come on up, like we said yesterday. We'll go for a swim, OK?" Carla asked him.

"OK. I'm coming. I'll be there soon. Don't leave!"

"Hahaha. Not to worry. I'm here. I'll be waiting for you."

With a joy he couldn't hide—it was written all over his face—he entered the hotel reception area. She winked at him. She had a guest she was dealing with. But soon, she finished with the hotel guest and, to Dieter's great joy, her shift was over.

"So how are you?" she asked. Why don't we go up to my room and have something to drink? We can put on our swim suits to go for a swim."

"Yes, let's! I already have my swim suit on, but let's go up. I want to hold you. I want you," he said, whispering in her ear. "Should we bring some coffee and water?"

"I have water and orange juice in my refrigerator, so there's no need. I've got coffee."

They sat for a while in Carla's room out on the balcony. Then Dieter went into the bathroom to wash off the salt from his earlier swim.

Carla made coffee and Dieter shouted to her from the bathroom. "Come on in, my sweet. I want you!"

"I'm coming," she replied. Throwing off her clothes, she joined him in the shower.

Later they lay in bed for a while to relax and only managed to get up to head for the beach for a swim two hours later. Fortunately, Dieter had the car.

The sea was crystalline, transparent and refreshing. They swam for some time, playing games and exchanging kisses in the magical waters.

After a while, they sat on the sand to dry. Dieter's body sank into her and she hugged him warmly, without clinging to him, since the sand there consisted of small pebbles. Ideal. The pebbles didn't get into their swimsuits or cling to their bodies or suits, so they weren't a problem.

Dieter felt happy, a feeling he hadn't had for a long time. He had even forgotten what it felt like. To be sure, he wasn't unhappy in Hannover, nor did he feel something was missing from his life. But that was because no object of desire had appeared to him. No woman had stirred up his interest. Of course, he was selective. And difficult. At the same time, he had lots of interests, so he didn't miss not having a relationship.

He had his music and some friends like Otto and other good musicians, mostly jazz musicians. He had the antique shop, his family, his reading and much more. Reading was of great interest to him, with his interests extending from novels to mathematics and physics. In brief, he didn't have the time to hang out at bars hoping to find a girlfriend, like many men of his age did. He had a full program with all his interests and so got along without the need for a girlfriend. Now, however, he was feeling emotionally gratified, with a sense of satisfaction deep within him, in the depths of his being.

They went back to Carla's hotel and, after washing off, sat on the veranda drinking iced coffee. "Frappe, they call it," Carla told him. A Greek "patent", she added, raising her eyebrows.

"It's wonderful! Refreshing," Dieter responded, nodding in agreement. They looked out at the sea in serenity. But their nirvana was interrupted by Carla's cell phone that began ringing insistently. She went into the room to answer it. It was Andreas.

"How are you, Carla? I've lost track of you. Are you OK?" he asked her.

"Yes. Everything is fine. I had a lot of things to do."

"Oh, good deal. I thought maybe you would come by the bar today and we could have a bite to eat together."

"I'd like to, but I can't today. I'm a little tired. I had a lot of work. But tomorrow would be good if you'd like. And what about you? How are your spirits?"

"Ah, I thought we'd spend time with the others. Never mind if you can't. Tomorrow. Give them a call yourself if you feel like it. As for me, it's like, you know. Sometimes up, sometimes down. The bar has some issues, but I'm working on them."

"OK. We'll talk tomorrow in person. Let's phone again this afternoon."

Returning to Dieter, she said, "it was Andreas. He wants to get together."

"Ah, and what did you tell him?"

"I told him I couldn't today. So tomorrow."

"Oh good, fortunately."

"Yes. I wasn't interested in seeing the others today."

"Me neither. I want to get my fill of you. Not in the mood to see the others, however much I enjoy them."

"Right."

"You know, we have to agree on what to tell the others," Dieter said cautiously, since he didn't like to fib, even if they were white lies. On the other hand, he didn't like having to account for his movements or respond to comments about what he was doing or planned to do.

He added, "Since I told Peter that we had gone together to see some houses, if he starts to ask, you have to know what to say. Since I told him that checking out some houses was all we were doing."

"Don't worry. I'll tell him that I'm looking for myself— everyone knows that already—and you took the opportunity to look for a small place for yourself, so it was worked out for us to go together. But I don't think Peter will dare question me. Don't think so."

"Alright. I hope he is not indiscreet. Naturally he questioned me, but he didn't get anything out of me."

"*Ha! What a situation.*"

"Yeah. He worked it back and forth and, despite his best efforts, didn't get anywhere. He knows that I like you. I told him that from the first moment I saw you. But for sure he doesn't think that anything has happened between us."

"Why not?"

"Because he knows I am cautious."

"But you weren't with me at all. To the contrary!"

"You swept me away, sweetheart. You made me bold because I couldn't do anything else. *I couldn't bear not having you.*"

Carla took his hand and whispered "fortunately". A bit later she said:

"Shall we stay here? I'd prefer it. I'm feeling tired...and with the shower. It was great, eh?"

"Perfect. Magical. And you were wonderful."

"So, what do you say. Shall we order something and eat in?"

"Agreed. But something light. What do you think?"

"Right."

They moved to the bed, where they spend the next couple of hours embracing and making love. Later, after their senses were sated, they decided it was time to eat. The ordered food and woofed down an omelet and a salad. Then they stretched out to watch a little television until they fell asleep.

Around seven in the morning, Dieter woke up. He got up from the bed slowly so as not to disturb his lover. He dressed quickly and left a note for Carla, who was deep asleep. Her beautiful back was exposed, so carefully and tenderly, he covered it up.

"My sweet," he wrote. "I am going to the port. I'll call you later. I didn't want to wake you up. You are so beautiful! I love you."

He went down to the port and parked the car a little further down so as not to make any noise. He crept into the studio apartment catlike so that Peter, who as snoring noisily, wouldn't notice. He laid down and in a while was overtaken by sleep.

But his sleep was turbulent and anxious. Maybe because of his exhaustion. Basically, his dreams were nightmarish, coming one after another. He was assaulted by terrifying and disgusting images creating frighteningly intense feelings, waking him up in a sweat.

His final dream, which he remembered vividly since it woke him up, was particularly intense. He was in an unknown land where the surface he was moving on was unstable and drab. Over his head, black birds were flying with large beaks, huge claws and aggressive intentions. He was wearing some rags that hung on him, torn and miserable. He was overcome by fear. He felt a cold sweat wash over him. He was looking for Peter, but shouted futilely in this barren land.

His shouts at some point had some effect, since he thought that, some distance away, he could see Peter as well as some other figures which, the closer they got, the more threatening they appeared. As they got closer, he saw that they weren't humans at all, but something else, something strange. They had heads like large fish and instead of hands, they had tentacles like jellyfish. He called for Peter to come quickly so they could leave and they could save themselves, but Peter made no response. He acted as if he was hypnotized.

When they got even closer, the creatures observed him carefully and he nearly fainted. Suddenly Peter, as if coming alive, shouted "Get out of here fast! Leave!" Dieter tried to run, but he couldn't, but at some moment a tornado came out of nowhere, swept him into its vortex and lifted him high into the air. And that's when he awoke.

He was sweaty and agitated.

23

If love were what the rose is,
And I were like the leaf,
our lives would grow together
In sad or singing weather.

A Match
Swinburne

Peter once again made earnest efforts to smoke out Dieter about his unusual excursions to find a house "to purchase", as he put it, but without results. Dieter held firm, keeping closed like a clam. Peter couldn't get a word out of him. So, like it or not, he abandoned the effort.

"You missed out. We had a great time yesterday with Otto and the other friends," Peter said. "We sat on the boat and had macaroni with a seafood sauce that Otto cooked. We drank some beer. What a great sailing boat that Beneteau is! Very high tech," he added emphatically. "They invited us to go for a swim today. Should we?"

"OK. Let's do. What time did you arrange for?"

"Well, right now, after breakfast. I'll bring along some

chips, beer and some sandwiches. We have bread and cheese here. I'll make them," he said eagerly.

They got ready and after a while arrived at their friends' boat. Soon they set sail for some beautiful beaches the sailors knew about. The day went by happily, mainly for Peter and their friends. Naturally, Dieter could only think about Carla. He was already missing her. But he couldn't just abandon his friend totally, or the others who, anyway, were good kids. He had at least to keep up appearances by engaging with the group, even though at this stage he was totally indifferent to the discussions about the boat and the other related male-oriented talk, since his mind was elsewhere--totally on Carla. He was present in body, but during the conversations, he participated without actually being engaged. Like a robot, mechanically, without thought.

Early in the afternoon, they returned to the port and tied up the boat. Already it was busy and lots of boats were trying to find a space. Fortunately, luck was with them.

Dieter's friends invited him politely to go with them the next day for a swimming trip, since they had had a good time and found the company enjoyable. But they also arranged to have a meal that evening at the port and asked Dieter and Peter if they were interested.

Peter naturally answered in the positive. But Dieter was aloof, since he hadn't talked to Carla yet. At the same time, he couldn't refuse. So, he found an excuse by needing to go to the supermarket supposedly to get something and discreetly left the group. As soon as he left the boat, he called Carla. Answering, she said, "Where are you? You left in the morning without waking me. Why? Are we going to meet today?"

"Let it be, my love. I've gotten involved with Peter and our sailor friends, that's why I didn't call you earlier. We took the boat out to take a swim. Peter has arranged to get together with them tonight for a meal. I can't avoid this, since most of them are my friends. In Hannover, I play music with Otto every ten days.

And he's a fine chap anyway. But I miss you, Carla. If you want, I'll come by later to see you. Are you going out with Andreas and the others? What did you arrange?"

"Yes. I'm going with them for a meal. That way, we'll escape the questioning. Better. So let's do it that way. I will be back at the hotel at eleven at the latest and you can come by. I'll send you a message when I leave the others for the hotel."

"Alright, my love. That's how we'll do it. I miss you."

"We'll talk later. Enjoy yourself."

Ending the call, Dieter went back to their room where, in the meantime, a cheerful Peter had returned. He had had a fantastic time, he told Dieter enthusiastically. "They're all great guys. Where were you hiding them for so long? We had a great time today, no?"

"Yes, yes. They are all great and a lot of fun," Dieter replied. But his mind was elsewhere: how he would take off that evening. He worked it out in his mind, wanting to escape Peter without comments and unwanted questions that might put him on edge and cause him to lose his temper. But there was no need for that, since the solution had been found.

24

For love is of sae mickle night,

That it all paines makis light

The Bruce

John Barbour

Taking the car and heading for the village, Dieter stole away quietly. Since Peter was with the sailor-friends, he didn't show much concern or ask annoying questions, but was satisfied his friend's excuse that he was "taking a stroll and would meet them later."

Before Peter knew what was happening, since he had thrown back a few beers, Dieter had taken off. Dieter was happy that he had escaped rather easily and headed towards Carla's hotel. It was five minutes before eleven and he had already gotten her message half an hour ago that she was returning to the hotel. So she should have already arrived.

"Carla! I'm here, my dear. Open up for me. In two minutes, I'll be outside your door."

Carla greeted him with a glass of white wine in her hand. "Welcome! I thought we'd have something to drink. What do you say?"

"Why not. Naturally. How are you, my sweet? How did things go?"

"Just fine. We ate early, fortunately, so I could get back early."

"How are the guys doing?"

"They're good. They asked after you. I told them I had seen you and that we had gone to see some houses....and that I imagine that tomorrow you would likely show up."

"Ah. So they didn't ask anything else?"

"No. Fortunately nothing. But I think that Antonis and Andreas are going to give you a call."

"Perfect. I'll tell them the same thing, without details of course."

"They are discreet. They won't put you on the spot."

"But I'm afraid that Peter...from what you said."

"Don't worry. He's with our sailor-friends right now and thankfully his attention is elsewhere. Just between us, they actually saved me," he said nodding his head back and forth.

"Tell me, my darling. How are you? I've been longing for you. What a beautiful woman you are! Today you are lovely. You look like the Madonna. For the first moment I saw you, that's what I saw. What have you been doing?"

"Nothing in particular. I was taking it easy."

"That's all?"

"Well, whatever you like. You've put me in the mood."

"Hahaha, great. Come close. I want to kiss and caress you. I missed you." He pulled her gently by the hand and embraced her, then caressed her hair, which he liked. It was soft and shiny. He pulled her towards him and her lips met his. His kiss expressed everything that he felt for her. He conveyed all the sweetness he felt for her and she melted. He undressed her tenderly and took her to the bed. As he began kissing her all over her body, she surrendered totally to him.

He threw off his clothes and fell onto the sheets, drawing her to him. Their union was absolute as he was overtaken by emotion.

"How much I missed you. I thought about you all day," he told her. "I love you, you know. I am certain I love you. It's the first time I've felt this way Carla, my love."

"You are sweet. You move me. I missed you too. And I also think that I love you," she whispered in his ear, kissing him.

Night passed amid unending caresses and kisses, over and over again. Embracing, exhausted by the intensity of their passion, they were finally overcome by sleep as it began to dawn.

25

The heart of the fool is in his mouth,

but the mouth of the wise man is in his heart.

Poor Richard's Almanac

Benjamin Franklin

Peter was happy. He had arranged with his new sailing friends to get together again for a swim. They had made the arrangement the night before, once Dieter had left, and he was eager to go find them. He planned to search for the shipwreck with his mask. He had the feeling that this time he would spot something.

Dieter had not shown up. The car was missing. "Strange", he thought. "What is my clever buddy up to?" He didn't find an answer, but almost immediately, Dieter arrived and walked into the room.

"I went to the supermarket to get some things and a lot of bottles of water, that's why I took the car," he said.

"Hmmm. Fine", said Peter, pretending that he bought the excuse.

SAILING THE WATERS OF IOS

He wasn't in the mood to argue, nor to ruin his good mood, with Dieter's excuses. In any case, he suspected what Dieter was up to. It had to do with the Italian woman. Naturally, he didn't believe, couldn't imagine, that things had gone so far. After all, he knew Dieter and how cautious he was. He wasn't so bold. He was a "don't touch me" type. "Very mysterious," he told himself. Not at all like himself. "But who cares about Dieter's antics? Let him do whatever he wants," he thought.

"So you woke up early, eh?" he said.

"Yes," Dieter answered nonchalantly, as he started to put the groceries away.

"What do you say about going with the guys for a swim today?" Peter said.

"Yes. Fine. Whatever you say. Did you arrange it yesterday?"

"Yes. You had gone....disappeared again."

"OK. Let's do it."

"I'm going out first to the shop to rent oxygen tanks for us both along with the other equipment, OK?" Peter said.

Dieter nodded positively, but one way or another, nothing could stop Peter.

26

The sea! the sea! The blue! The fresh, the ever free!

The Sea

B.W. Procter

They went to their friends' yacht and, since the weather was very good, they decided to set sail quickly from the port. Otto was in high spirits, but in fact everyone was in a jovial mood. They exchanged jokes and teased one another, with Peter's jokes making him a prime participant, since he knew a slew of jokes and delivered them rapid-fire. They also discussed classic works about sailing, like the novel *Kon Tiki*. It turned out that few of them knew that the book was initially rejected for publication by the copy editor of the publishing house because he thought it was boring, only to pull out his hair later when the book flew off the shelves.

They finally arrived at a beach and anchored offshore so as to avoid others anchoring near them. They did a lot of swimming and gazed around in the deep with their masks while Peter, once again, caught some octopus, as well as a large fish that turned out to be a dusky grouper. Overjoyed, he showed his catch around and everyone agreed that they should cook it on board.

Helmut assumed the cooking duties. The menu included tomato salad in olive oil, avocado and parsley, while Helmut cooked the octopus as directed by Peter, who had learned Haris' ingenious recipe. Following Peter's instructions, Helmut added a little seawater. The fish was grilled and was large enough to feed everyone.

They ate and drank abundant quantities. With spirits high, Peter revealed his secret. Inebriated, he began to "sing", as they say, reciting the story told him by Timothy. Dieter was stunned but sat silent, while the others showed interest and urged the drunken Peter to tell them more. Peter spilled all the beans and, drunk like he was, laughed loudly and enthusiastically. The center of everyone's attention, he exuded self-importance, reflecting the vanity that was characteristic of him.

Dieter didn't speak, since he had given an oath of silence to Peter. As for the others, they wanted to learn all of the details and were very interested in learning where their two friends had already searched. At some point, Peter sobered up, but it was too late. However, he didn't show any regret over his confession. To the contrary, he said it would be better if they all searched for the treasure together, since that would make it easier to extract the treasure from the sea, as well as sell it afterwards. As for the profit he thought it would yield, they could divide it up fairly into equal shares. There would be enough for everyone, he declared confidently.

It was logical that it would be easier for them to deal with the issue as a group. Dieter gave his assent. Anyway, the treasure was the last thing he was now interested in. Nor did he have any appetite to search for it or to think about how they would sell it, should they find it and retrieve it from the sea. *If that ever did happen.* Since, at best, he expected that they would find some broken jugs or amphorae.

"Just imagine! Dieter, what's your opinion?" Otto asked.

"I agree. I have no objections. But don't take it as a given...that something will be found, I mean," Dieter answered enigmatically. But the group of young men were inclined to believe and, as a result, took a group decision to look for the treasure again with greater organization. They laid out plans over where to search further. The discussion gained momentum. Otto, who loved to tease, threw in a number of jokes, suggesting that "in the end maybe they wouldn't find anything", distancing him from Peter, who was certain about the treasure.

"It exists, I'm sure. Timothy left no doubt. And he told me because he found me very likeable and was himself now very old. He wasn't joking. That's not what he was like. The issue, however, is how we are going to raise it from sea and how we are going to ship it and to where. And after that, the issue, of course, is how to sell what we found," he said nodding his head.

27

O villain, villain, smiling, damned villain!

Hamlet

Shakespeare

A t the equipment shop, Loumir was overly eager in attending to Peter.

"I missed you and wondered if you had left....I was thinking that maybe they went to another island," he said bluntly.

"No. We're still here."

"You don't want an inflatable today?"

"No. It won't be necessary, since we're going with some friends in a sailing boat, the Matilde."

"Ah yes," Loumir answered, adding: "You're going again to observe fish in the depths?"

"Yes, something like that," Peter said nervously, starting to get anxious about Loumir's questions.

"Just give me the equipment we had before," Peter said hastily.

Loumir searched for the things Peter asked for, glancing back stealthily at the German from the shelves and acting as if he was having trouble finding the equipment Peter wanted. He was trying to figure out what Peter was looking for. He was not at all convinced that the Germans continued simply to be interested in the fish of the deep. At last, he brought the equipment to Peter, who paid and left the store.

Not wasting any time, the Albanian spoke on his cell phone with a friend and they called another member of their group, a Greek, Vangelis, whose street name was Vangos. He was a vagabond and ex-prisoner who hung out with them. They agreed to go out on a rubber raft to follow Peter and his friends *in order to see where they were going and figure out what they were looking for.*

With the boss in Athens on business, Loumir closed the shop early and the three took the raft and headed out quickly from the port. Using binoculars, they followed the sailing boat Peter had boarded. They found it easily and followed it with the binoculars from a distance. At some point, they saw the Germans dive into the sea along with their friends. There were now four of them in the water. Others had remained on board. They counted three.

"Seems to me there are a lot of them," said Vangos, the Greek. He was a dark-skinned man with a beard and wild features, short and stocky.

"We probably need to take along some weapons, a pistol and maybe a rifle wouldn't be bad," the Albanian, Loumir, said without hesitation.

"For sure. I'll take it on myself," said Vangos, the gangster.

Sneaky and cautiously, like hyenas, they spent a fair amount of time following the Germans. At some point, Vangos nudged Loumir, who was next to him: "They're coming out now. Let' see. Did they catch any fish?"

"Look carefully," Loumir said. "Let me know. I don't see so far without the binoculars."

Emver—the third member of the party—was sitting quietly following the other two. Then he said, "Hey. What do you think they're looking for?"

"Could be anything. Maybe a shipwreck. They could have information about some treasure, a cache of coins from pirates," Loumir said meaningfully.

"Yes. Gold vases and artifacts. Pirate treasure," Vangos said emphatically. "Bayioko, bikikinia....I'm talking about money, get it, dummy, gold and coins?"

"Hmmm. Alright. Are there shipwrecks from pirate ships here?" Emver asked, receiving an angry reply from Loumir.

"Yeah, you idiot. There are. Everyone says so!"

Three hours went by as the watched carefully, but without seeing anything that answered their questions. But the fact that the Germans were looking for something in the sea focused their attention. "Let's go back," said Loumir quickly turning the raft around and returning to the port. They decided to trail them again, but this time they planned to bring weapons with them.

28

There's nothing half so sweet in life

As love's young dream

Love's Young Dream

Thomas Moore

"Peter, it was a good outing today. But don't expect you are going to find the treasure with Timothy's statues, my friend," Dieter said when they got to their room.

"Fine, so say you. But I'm certain. How to say? I feel it. Still if you don't want to follow, run around with your Italian girlfriend. Seems like she is leading you around by the nose. But our friends believe what I'm saying."

"It's not that I don't believe you. And I hope you find something, even if not much. But a great shipwreck, statues in the deep. What can I say. It seems to me impossible," Dieter said condescendingly.

"Not to worry, Dieter. I will keep trying. I owe it to myself. I'm going to keep to the chase. I'm sure there is something. And you know what? I like all this searching. The adventure. The drama of the chase. Not to mention that our friends are enjoying it too."

"As you like, my friend. But I'm going to the village to see the others. Don't come along. Stay here with Otto. Enjoy yourself."

"Yes. That's it. Take the car if you like," Peter said, with exaggerated generosity.

Relieved Dieter grabbed the opportunity and, after taking a shower, dressed quickly in jeans and a black shirt. Leaving the apartment quickly, he headed towards the car. Shortly later, he reached Chora, turned off the engine at the side of the road and called Carla on his cell phone:

"Hi, my love. It's Dieter!"

"Dieter? Which Dieter?" she said teasingly.

"I know you're kidding me. It's your beloved Dieter!"

"Haha, so you didn't take the bait. Where are you? Are you coming by here?"

"Yes. I'm on my way. In a few minutes I'll be there with you. Will you come out to greet me? Maybe you want to stay where you are?"

"Come on by and we'll figure it out. I'll wait for you outside."

In seven minutes, in fact, Dieter had arrived at the hotel where his lover was waiting for him. "How are you, my love? I've been missing you," he told her.

She grabbed his arm and together they went to her room. They decided to stay in Carla's room and to go out later for a drink.

"Andreas called me and said he'd be at the bar with Antonis. He asked us to drop by. Should we go?"

"Of course. Let's go!"

But their need to be together by themselves made them change their plans. Once again, they slept together. They forgot about the outing. Morning found them embracing in bed. Carla woke up first. She had gotten cold because the sheet had fallen off the bed. Dieter noticed her and also got up. "My love, what time is it? You're awake?"

"Yes. I got cold and it woke me up."

"Me too. Should we get some more sleep? Are you tired?"

They slept for another hour and at seven, Dieter got up, dressed slowly so as not to waken Carla, kissed her and left the room, closing the door quietly behind him.

He arrived at the port in less than 15 minutes. He entered the room slowly, where Peter was doing his classic snoring. He too laid down to sleep. But it was a heavy sleep, maybe due to his being dead tired, with a series of anxiety dreams.

Rising from bed, he called Carla as soon as he could, but was startled by her reception. He realized she was busy and couldn't speak freely because she was at the front desk dealing with someone.

"I'll call you in a while," she said, hastily ending the call.

Dieter felt concerned, but Carla soon called him back.

"What happened, my love? You seemed sort of...what was going on?"

"A lot. Forget it."

"Such as? Like what?"

"Andy has returned suddenly. He came by in a fury and says he wants to get together again."

"What?"

"Yes. Just as I said."

Peter momentarily lost it, but then said: "And you, what

did you say?"

"What could I say? I told him that that couldn't happen....that I am now with someone else, someone I like a lot."

Dieter's heart returned to normal, since for a moment, when he heard the news, it had frozen.

"And he accepted that?" he finally managed to say.

"Naturally. What could he do? He was the one who broke off the relationship. He had grown weary, he had said. He had maybe found someone else. I don't know and I don't care. Fortunately, it happened that way and I was left free for you. Maybe I should erect a statue for him."

"And now, what's going to happen?" Dieter asked anxiously.

"Nothing. I settled accounts with him and we are done. And he shouldn't have any hopes because there is no way that we will be together again."

"Are you sure?"

"He doesn't interest me at all. It's as if he never existed! Harsh, but that's how it is."

"So where is he now?" Dieter managed to ask.

"He'll come back to the hotel, I imagine. I don't know. Nor did I ask him. He told me he was going to Santorini tomorrow. That's where he came from, it seems and he came here to find me. The man is crazy, I tell you."

"Fine. Forget about it."

"Forget it. It's the past and, in fact, it's long past," Carla said humorously.

"I'm coming by there now," Dieter said.

"Come on by!"

So they met once again and, after once more declarations of love and passion, they ended up in bed, where they spent the whole afternoon until the late evening.

For Dieter, Peter was the last thing on his mind.

29

We were the first that ever burst

Into that silent sea.

The Ancient Mariner

S. T. Coleridge

Over the next few days, the German friends spent their time searching in the sea for Timothy's treasure. They had gone to the store with the nautical equipment and scuba diving tanks. There, Dieter's friends, Otto and the other four, rented suits and tanks, to Loumir's great surprise, as he rushed to serve them.

Loumir tried to strike up a conversation with them, but without luck. They all answered in generalities, which, of course, confirmed his suspicions that they were looking for something. Of course, he knew that already, since he had followed them earlier. *He got together his own gang and arranged to again follow the Germans, which they were able to do since Loumir's boss was fortunately still away on business.* This time, they brought weapons along in order to be ready if more drastic action was needed. Loumir had something with him and found Vangos, the other "flower" of the gang. Emver followed along, but he was innocent of such doings.

Despite following from a distance with binoculars and with their feelings at a high pitch, they didn't observe anything. The Germans had not even gotten fish out of the sea, despite diving into the water for hours and despite the efforts they were apparently making. "They aren't even catching fish, so what are they spending so many hours in that place for?" asked Vangos.

"I told you so," Loumir said emphatically. "For sure they're looking for something, for a treasure. I'm telling you, they are looking for gold coins or the like. You should listen to me!"

For a few days it went on like this, until Emver started to get resentful. "If we don't find anything today, I'm not coming tomorrow," he told the others.

"OK. We'll see," an irritated Loumir answered, making a grimace that made his rugged face even uglier. But, to his good fortune, that hot afternoon, he observed some unusual movement on the deck of the Beneteau. "Well, laddies, now we'll see what you're up to," he boomed. "We'll see what are they looking so hard for."

Happy with this development, he pressed the binoculars to his eyes and forehead, watching intensely while commenting. He was overjoyed, certain that they were looking for something important. Something that would make them rich! "You think you have gotten by Loumir? No way. I'm on to you," he boastfully said again and again.

Next to him, Vangos also followed like a hyena and Emver, sitting without binoculars, listened to their babble.

Meanwhile, the Germans were moving nervously around the deck and it seemed something important was happening, since they were making gestures and it appeared that they were engaged in doing something. They dove into the sea and emerged again and again. Loumir was fixed to his binoculars trying to understand what was going on. "Shhh. Don't talk. I want to focus on what they are doing," he told the other two.

Vangos, with his own binoculars, followed like a predator ready to attack. Emver followed the others silently. He didn't dare say anything since they were constantly putting him down. So he sat quietly.

At some moment, Loumir broke the silence, saying, "This evening, let's go and search the spot where they are now. I am certain that the whities have found something. Haha! We'll take it ourselves. We are going to raise the gold coins from the sea! Get ready to be rich, my boys!"

"Good then, let's leave and come back again tonight along with our diving equipment," Vangos said. Gathering up their things, they left. Arriving at the port, they went to Loumir's place and worked out their plan in detail.

That same night, now well organized with suits and tanks, underwater flashlights, weapons and spearguns, along with nets and bags to take the treasure out of the sea, they launched the rubber raft and headed to the spot where the Germans had been that afternoon.

"Are you sure about this is the place where the Germans were looking?" Emver asked Loumir hesitantly.

"Yes, of course. Totally certain. I used that rock as a signpost and checked the map. We're here," Loumir said, while Vangos said sharply, "We're here, Emver. You think we don't know what we're looking for? Don't be hassle!"

Following their plan, Loumir and Vangos would enter the sea to do the search, since they were good swimmers and were able to dive with the oxygen tanks, while Emver would stand by on the raft. And so it happened. Emver would be on the lookout for anyone who showed up and signal them with the underwater flashlight. He had been properly equipped. Anyway, they felt certain that everything would go well and that they had nothing to fear.

A little after midnight, the three had arrived at the spot where they needed to search. The two men donned their suits, fixed the oxygen tanks on their backs, and put on their swim fins. They also took with them an air-powered speargun with a flashlight and were now ready to dive into the black waters. The night was dark. Loumir dived in first. Then, Vangos after a minute. The water splashed when Vangos dove in and was then silent.

Emver sat on the raft and lit up a cigarette. It was just what he needed at the moment. He inhaled deeply, so strongly that it burnt his lungs. Running through his head was the idea that he would become rich and he began to think about what he would do with the money from the treasure. For sure there would be gold coins, since his friends, who knew about these things said so. He would go back to Tirana and buy an apartment. Then he would go to his village to get his mother and sister to take them to see it. *How happy they would be.* Then, he would buy a car, *preferably a Mercedes*, and he would have his own mode of transportation. So much for his bicycle, which he was sick and tired of.

He lit another cigarette to pass the time. The sea was quiet. Not a sound. He took a look around. But there wasn't anything nearby. No light.

A fair amount of time passed and there was no sign of his two friends. He started to wonder and get a little worried. "So what happened to them?" he thought. "They're taking some time, it seems." However, he trusted them, since he had confidence in their skill. "*They must have found something. That's why they're so late.*" That thought calmed him. He smoked three more cigarettes as he waited. Still nothing. Not a sound. He used the flashlight to see what was going on. But he didn't see or hear anything. Now he really began to get worried.

He got antsy. "What the devil is going on? Where are they? What happened? Maybe something went wrong. Bah. They must have found something. At any moment, they will show up and come to the surface." Again, however, he didn't hear anything or see any light or anything moving in the deep. Total quiet.

He didn't know how to swim and had no experience in searching in the sea. Nor did he have a suit, but even then, he was totally without experience in dealing with the sea. They had brought him along just to serve as a guard. An extra pair of eyes and hands.

Much time passed and his anxiety began to grow. Nearly three hours must have passed. That was a lot. They had told them that, at most, they would be about an hour. That was their estimate, and they knew what they were talking about.

He drank some water and tried to calm down. Then, he remembered that somewhere in his bag he had a bottle of Coca Cola. He opened it and drank that too. He was thirsty. The Coca Cola quenched his thirst. He waited a bit more.

He then had three more cigarettes, one after the other. And still nothing. Not a sign. He leaned towards the sea holding on to the rope along the side of the inflatable raft. He saw nothing. Heard nothing.

He began feeling desperate and didn't know what to do. He got panicky. But he still sat and waited. What else could he do? There was no alternative. Here in the remote waters of Ios.

His anxiety peaked. He was overcome by panicky thoughts. What would happen if something bad had happened to his friends? How would he deal with it? And if they caught him and considered him to be responsible. And what if they put him in jail and then expelled him from the country? That was the good scenario. *The bad scenario would be if he were charged as responsible and they nailed him for it.*

Such thoughts unnerved him. "No, no. Nothing will

happen. I shouldn't think negatively." He sat again in the center of the raft and tried to calm down. Far away on the horizon, the first rays of dawn began to appear. "Ah. So much time has passed and they haven't given a sign of life. What should I do now?" he thought. Unable to reach a conclusion, he decided to wait a little longer. It wasn't quite daylight yet.

At some distance, he thought he heard the sound of an engine. He sat up to try and hear something, but the sound disappeared. Nothing again. Now the sky began to get light. His anxiety was driving him crazy. He was seized by a feeling of hopelessness. "What fool I am", he thought. "Why did I want to get caught up in this? Why did I get involved in Loumir's megalomania? Why didn't I just sit tight. What would happen now?"

He was literally terrified. He looked into the sea. Total panic. "I'll wait a little longer and then what? Go to the police? What can I say, if they hold me responsible? What should I do?" he thought, and kept thinking, but got nowhere. He was soaked in a cold sweat and overtaken by fear. He made an effort to put his head into the water, turning to the side of the raft and holding again onto the rope in order to see. But what could he see? Something, anything, but then nothing. No sign of the two.

He decided to return. He'd put the raft back where they started and then see what might happen later. Maybe they had swum back, if they had gotten lost and just swam back. If they hadn't returned, then he would go to the police, or at least consider it.

Had anyone seen them leaving the port in the middle of the night? He raised the anchor, started up the engine and headed towards the harbor. He arrived quickly. There wasn't a soul around. "Good deal," he thought. "I'm lucky." He tied up the raft and quickly got out, taking his bag and the bags of the other two, with their clothing and sandals, and headed rapidly towards the room where he was staying by the taverna. They had rented it to him cheaply. He didn't run into anyone on the road. Everyone was sleeping. "Great," he thought.

In his room, he lay down on the hard mattress and began thinking. He decided to stay there until noon or maybe the afternoon, in case they showed up. "One way or another, Loumir's boss was still on business in Athens, and as for Vango, no one would be looking for him. He had been released from prison recently, as far as he knew from what Loumir told him. "Good again. They wouldn't be looking for him."

30

We may not have chosen the time,

but the time has chosen us.

John
Lewis

Police chief Perdikaris was sitting at his desk. Tired, in fact exhausted, he was reading through a pile of police department documents. Again there had been arguments last night at the bar, fights between inebriated young punks, once again he had to be on the move in the middle of the night. They had three in holding cells and his assistants were once again overwhelmed.

The budget was not enough to cover their needs and chances were nil that he could add any personnel to the police station. Headquarters had effectively cut them off. "Do what you can. There's no money. Get by with what you have," they told him. "End of story. Don't ask us over and over. There's no money. Forget what former George Papandreou had to say, recalling the Greek prime minister's famous words just before Greece's recent economic crisis that '*money exists*'".

He was tired of the island, since every day it was something else, especially during the summer. For him, the summer months were hell. A beautiful island, "magnificent", but he had gotten weary. Very weary.

"Let's see when my transfer will come through," he reflected. He was so nostalgic for his hometown in Laconia. Its clean air, its mountains, in particular the Taygetos, which he worshipped, the green, the sound of the sheep and goat bells. The smells of the forest, of the land, of the hay. His village was Georgitsi, a mountain village of the Taygetos, with its magnificent stone houses. The water flowing bountifully from the springs was clean. Everything was peaceful, quiet, intimate. How on earth did he end up on this island?

From his balcony in his village, he could see the mountains across the way, specifically the majestic Parnon, as well as the Pelana valley below, and from there the eye reached all the way to Sparta. Magnificent, beloved colors. Parnon, the other great mountain, just opposite his balcony. How much he missed that view. And now he, for the good of the department, was in the middle of the Aegean.

But his transfer never came through. Meanwhile, the needs had gotten larger. His colleagues were constantly complaining and everyone's nerves were on edge.

"We need new vests. Will we have to pay for them again?" they asked. "And our guns. They are also outdated. We can't go on working like this. It just can't be, sir."

"Perdikaris, what can he do?" the unfortunate police chief thought to himself, addressing himself in the third person. "Where can he find the funds? From where?" Furthermore, he was not a weapons maker. Since his own salary had been cut during the economic crisis of the last several years, he had an economic problem. He wanted to get some new shoes, but was still thinking about it. Even that. He didn't make a decision. Let it be for a while still. They'll hold up, he thought. Patience.

He had grown weary, and he was right. But what could he do? No solution appeared. The island was filled with tourists and the shop owners were waiting for the summer for business to pick up. A difficult balance. "Everything in this life is hard. Unending problems. Something was always happening."

His job never left him with a quiet moment. And now, along with the rest, a new incident had taken place. He had just been informed by his colleagues that some Albanian had appeared and told them that two individuals, one Albanian and one Greek he had gone fishing with never emerged from the water, but "were lost in the sea," he said.

He waited for them in the ship, "but after many hours had passed with no sign of life, he didn't know what to do except to return back," the policeman's assistant mumbled glumly. "He didn't know how to swim in order to dive in too. They had brought him along just to guard the boat, an inflatable dinghy that they had." It belonged to Manolis, who had the store at the port that had oxygen tanks for diving, they told him.

Perdikaris was upset. Along with everything else on his mind, this had to happen too. "Good lord," he thought, "couldn't this have happened a while later? Did it have to happen now? Damn it."

He took a swallow of Greek coffee that had gone cold on his desk and got ready to interview the Albanian. His colleagues had told him to wait in an office. Perdikaris got up from his desk, adjusted the shirt that was clinging to him because of the heat and sweat. "Heat, an unbearable situation," he droned under his breath. "The air conditioning. Old and performing poorly. We'll see when we can replace it."

In quick moves, he walked assuredly through a gloomy

hallway painted in a washed-out sea-blue color, reaching the office where a frightened Emver was sitting. Perdikaris opened the door of the office aggressively. Emver's eyes rolled in fright, tensing up in the chair.

"What do we have here? Who are you? What's your name," Perdikaris said in a booming voice.

"Emver Rakipi, sir. I work in the taverna, in the kitchen, the taverna at the port," Emver said, his voice trembling.

"OK. So tell me, what exactly happened?"

"We went fishing, the two friends, I mean, and I don't know how to swim or how to fish, and they never came out of the water. I waited...."

"When did this happen?"

"Last night. Loumir and Vangos. They were friends."

"What time, and where did the incident happen?" the police officer asked aggressively.

"We went late. Midnight. Twelve-ten or so."

"OK, OK. Where exactly did you go?"

"Beyond the harbor, up to the right about a mile and a half, somewhere around there....me not know, sir", he said haltingly.

"Try to remember something nearby. What was close by?"

"I don't know. It's the first time I've been there. It was dark. Night. I don't know...I didn't see."

"Alright. So what happened there? Come on, speak," the officer said, pressing him.

"They dived into the sea and I was waiting and waiting for them, but they never showed up...Gone, in the sea...nighttime. I waited, I called and waited..."

"And then? What else?"

"Nothing else, nothing. As soon as it got light, I left and

came here."

"OK, but tell me, why were you going fishing at night?"

"I don't know sir...Don't know...I can't swim.

"What were you fishing for? Did you have oxygen tanks? Were you looking for something? What did they tell you?"

"They didn't tell me anything, I don't know. I was in the boat, to guard the boat. I don't know."

"The other one, who was he? Did you know him? Where was he from?"

"Vangos. I don't know. He was a friend of Loumir from Athens...."

"Did they tell you why they were going with tanks? What did they say to you?"

"Nothing. I don't know, honest! Loumir didn't tell me anything. He just said to come along to help."

Right. What else do you know? How long have you known Loumir? Did you meet him here?"

"Yes, here."

"And? What kind of fellow was he? What did he want, I mean?"

"He was good. He wanted to go fishing. I don't know anything else."

"So he just wanted you to sit on the boat?"

"Yes, that's all."

"Hmmm."

"Yes."

"So you're kidding me, right?"

"No, I'm not kidding you!"

"Are you pulling my leg?"

"No, no, it's the truth. I don't know. I don't know anything."

"Great. Then you can sit in jail until you remember!"

"But I don't know."

Perdikaris grimaced as if he didn't believe anything Emver was telling him. His patience was exhausted, it was hot and the air conditioning was faulty. That one's old too. Where can we find money for it!

He called for his assistant in a loud voice. "Manouso, come on in and take him away." As soon as his assistant showed up, he said in a bored voice, "Put him in the jail cell for today and the next and maybe he'll remember what in the devil they were doing out there."

The assistant took Emver, his head bowed, and led him to the cell, urging him to "refresh his memory, fess up and maybe avoid prison."

Emver was petrified. He followed along without resistance. Entering the cell, he curled up in a corner.

31

He cursed him in living,

He cursed him in dying!

The Jackdaw of Rheims

R. H. Barham

In the days that followed, the Coast Guard became involved in the investigation. They went to the place where Loumir and Vangos disappeared, but didn't manage to find anything. Not the slightest trace of the two vanished men. Nothing at all.

Emver remained in his jail cell and was interrogated daily, but didn't contribute anything to the investigation. They gave him sandwiches and coffee and informed his boss at the taverna that he would be held at the police station until further notice.

Perdikaris became engaged in the case and tried to understand how it was, if they had drowned at that location, that their bodies had not shown up there or nearby. Residents living nearby were informed to be on the lookout. Meanwhile, the Coast Guard continued its search. But not even a single clue showed up anywhere. Not even a piece of clothing. It was as if nothing had happened.

Perdikaris suspected that Emver had possibly gotten into a fight with the other two and during the fight had murdered them and then buried their bodies somewhere. He discarded the story about fishing. Still, nothing came of it. Despite persistent questioning and interrogation, Emver hadn't said anything that would suggest anything like that. Meanwhile, the Coast Guard, for its part, kept Perdikaris updated daily on any findings.

After a week, the investigation ceased. The case remained unsolved. Perdikaris continued to hold Emver, hoping maybe he would break, but he couldn't do so for long. He had to release him and let the case take a different turn.

Meanwhile, the story had gotten around the island and, predictably, reached the ears of Andreas and Antonis, who shared it the others in the group. Carla learned about it at the hotel and mentioned it to Dieter who told Peter who, in turn, told the others.

32

Morality is a private and costly luxury.

The Education of Henry Adams

Henry Adams

Dead tired, Carla was sitting on her bed just after finishing her shift at the front desk. A horde of teenage German tourists had arrived, a group of youngsters who wanted information about everything, as well as a French woman who needed first aid because she had been stung by a wasp. That was the most stressful.

After dealing with it all, Carla arrived exhausted at her room and sat in bed to recover from her taxing day. She was in pieces. Before she had a chance to undress, the telephone rang. It was Dieter who wanted to know when they would meet.

"I just finished work and I'm dead tired. I'll call you back when I've had a shower and I've gotten it back together."

"Fine, my sweet," he said hastily. Dieter understood from the tone of her voice that she was in fact exhausted from fatigue. The two agreed to go later for food at a little taverna they both liked. As for the rest of the circle of friends, Carla spoke with Andreas and said she would see him at the bar after the meal.

And so it happened. After the evening meal, Carla and Dieter passed by Andreas' bar to see him and have a drink. The topic of discussion was the drowning of the two fishermen in a region about a mile-and-a-half north of the harbor. Dieter didn't mention that it was near to where the Germans were hunting for Timothy's treasure. How could he let that be known? He had taken a vow of silence. So he didn't mention either the place or that they had gone there to swim. That place, anyway, was not approachable except by boat. No one else would go there. He had no appetite for getting into this conversation, especially because he felt indifferent about the whole issue.

Andreas was in high spirits that evening. He told them stories about the years when he visited Ios as a youth, about the bars and discos there that had left their mark, such as Homer's Cave in the village and the Ios Club on the hill, as well the unusual bar, the Rolling Elephant, the first large one which, he told them, was amazing. As he was telling them these colorful old stories, then suddenly was a loud boom, a roaring noise, deafening and terrible. The foundations of the building began shaking, turning their cheerful mood into panic and fear.

"Earthquake, earthquake! Everyone outside!" Andreas shouted, tugging them by their clothes to leave the bar and head for the village square. "Ah, what's this again? This quake is stronger than the first one, I think," Andreas said with Dieter nodding in agreement. Carla was the only one who was calm, since she was accustomed to quakes.

Such was the case, they learned shortly later. On television, the news came from the Athens Observatory and the Geodynamics Institute, the source of the most authoritative estimates, that the earthquake had been somewhat larger than the first, with an epicenter slightly to the west. The experts said it was too early to predict further shocks and recommended that people be alert and take safety precautions. The experts weren't sure yet if the quake was the primary one. Maybe yes, maybe no. That would become clear in the coming hours and days, based on seismic tracking. "There is seismic activity in the region", the experts announced and just left the issue there.

Carla and Dieter decided to go back to the hotel to sleep and Andreas closed the bar and went home. So they said their goodbyes and agreed to meet the next day. Meanwhile, Dieter informed Peter, who was with the other Germans, about their experiences with the quake.

"Yes, and we were pretty strongly affected here too," was the response from Peter, who was mildly traumatized. "Do you want to come by here? What do you say?"

"Not yet. Later. Aren't you with Otto and the others?"

"Yeah, no problem. Stay as long as you like!" Peter answered, who fortunately had accepted the fact of Dieter's relationship with Carla. He ceased asking a lot of questions, mainly because he was with his German friends, who were set on searching with him for the treasure. So no problem!

Meanwhile, everyone had learned about the drowning of the two spearfishermen and the fruitless searches by the Coast Guard over the several last days. As for Peter and his friends, it was decided to begin their hunt for the treasure again, if not the next day, then soon after.

33

Believing where we cannot prove.

In Memoriam

Tennyson

It was a brilliant day with a calm sea and a light breeze, perfect for a quiet trip on the yacht belonging to the Germans. Peter and the others had arranged to go for a swim and search for the treasure, having made the necessary preparations the day before.

Peter was enthusiastic about finally renewing their search. This time he felt that the moment of discovery was close. He was convinced that something was going to happen. Something decisive for the rest of his life. He couldn't wait! He was already making plans for what he would do with the money after selling the treasure. He was certain that he would become rich and could then do anything he wanted with the money. He just needed a little luck. Just a slight push from the goddess of good fortune.

He planned on buying a large sailing ship that was modern with a lot of conveniences. He liked the Beneteau owned by his companions. He would buy something like that, he thought. He would go on cruises with his friends. That's where his thoughts traveled. He would go around the world. He would go on holiday for at least a couple of years until he got tired of it. He was very certain that the treasure was there waiting for him.

34

Farewell, remorse:

all good to me is lost;

Evil, be thou my good

Paradise Lost

Milton

Peter put on his wetsuit, adjusted the oxygen tanks with Otto's help and dived into the water. Ahead of him, Walter had already dived in, swimming around the boat in order to check on the anchor. They dived smoothly in the blue waters until, in the depths, they found a rocky region. Fish were swimming around them in the deep, some very large, but they had no interest at the moment in fishing.

Peter looked around carefully, hoping to detect some trace of the shipwreck, but couldn't find any. Then suddenly, just as he was getting ready to surface, he observed a fissure in a large boulder which gave him the impression that maybe it was hiding something. It appeared interesting and might lead somewhere. He signaled Walter to wait where he was until he had a chance to check out exactly what was there.

Not hesitating, he moved closer to see the spot better when, suddenly, pushing aside the seaweed with his gloved hands, he detected a widening in the fissure. He got closer and discovered to his surprise that the opening appeared large enough for him to enter. Pushing through the water with his swim fins to gain momentum, he turned onto his side in order to slide more easily into the recess in the boulder.

It was indeed a passageway. Advancing cautiously, grasping the walls with his hands carefully to avoid ripping his wetsuit, he managed to enter the boulder that suddenly opened onto a path to an underground cave. Swimming down slowly, he was led to another smaller cave and there in the distance, he saw something very strange: a somewhat larger entrance to the cave. He made his way quickly, and now at one end something looking like part of a mast, covered with shells, stood out from the sand. He cautiously approached the spot and, digging with his hands, he discovered, after pushing away the sand, that something was underneath. Wasting no time, he realized that, most likely, this was the shipwreck Timothy had told him about. But how had it gotten there, so deep inside the rock formation?

Emerging quickly, he looked for Walter who was waiting just outside the fissure in the boulder. The two of them on carefully entered the opening and reached the last cave at the point where they could see the protrusion that was likely the remnants of the mast. It indeed must have been the shipwreck, buried in the deep by sand all around. Walter gestured to Peter with his hand. The question now was how old it was. Was it really the one that Timothy had talked about or maybe something more recent? That remained to be seen.

Gesturing to each other, they agreed to surface and discuss the matter with the others. In any case, they had been in the deep for some time. They rose slowly and carefully to the surface and, poking their heads above the water, swam rapidly towards the ship. The others were sitting and drinking coffee in the cockpit and were having a general discussion about wind and water, about the women they loved, about the island of Ios and its beauties, and, of course, about Peter and the shipwreck.

As soon as they took off their suits, the two treasure-hunters sat at the main table. Drinking coffee and eating biscuits and cheese, they began to tell the others the story in detail. They followed in surprise and shouts of delight.

"So really! Bravo, Peter. You were right after all!" Otto and Hans shouted while the others laughed loudly. Then, after their initial excitement, they started to evaluate the situation, reaching the conclusion that, most likely, the earthquake of a few days ago, and maybe others, had shifted the seabed beneath the rock formation along with the shipwreck. After considering all aspects of the issue, they decided to dive in groups of three to see what they had found. For certain, it was something important.

And so they did. First Peter, Hans and Otto dived and next Walter and the others. Their initial impression was that, in fact, something had happened there, but how they could see what was underneath what was already visible, and how they could bring anything to the surface was another matter. They would need to bring some specialized tools to do some digging, as well as some large sacks to put in any objects they dug up. Walter, Peter, Otto and Hans would assume those tasks, while the others would deal with the other complications. As for Dieter, who wasn't present, he would be informed later by Peter. Such was their agreement.

35

Forever, brother, hail and farewell.

In perpetuum, frater, ave atque vale.

Ode
Catullus

Perdikaris sat in his office with a cup of coffee staring abstractly at the wall across from him. He was thinking about the two characters who had disappeared. No progress had been made. Emver hadn't said anything that went beyond his initial statement and, with a heavy heart, Perdikaris was forced to let him free after a few days. The two divers didn't emerge from the sea, nor were their remains found. That's where things stood.

So what had happened? An enigma. Still, something inside told him that it wasn't possible for them to vanish just like that. They weren't just some vagrants. Perdikaris had done some research and determined that Vangos was an ex-convict. No one was looking for him, but from the ramblings of Emver,

Perdikaris had reached that conclusion. But where were their bodies? Were they eaten by the fish? After only one day, only hours after their disappearance, it seemed hard to believe that there was no trace of them. Not even a shred of clothing! Emver, that no-good, was hiding something, but it was strange that he didn't say a word beyond his original statement.

Maybe the Albanian was not so dumb after all, thought Perdikaris. He approached his interrogation from different angles, but couldn't get anything out of him. To be sure, Perdikaris was a professional with some wins to his name. Some months earlier, his team had an important success: They managed to break up a narcotics ring that dealt mostly with cocaine and had been operating on the island the last three years.

It had taken a lot of effort. Perdikaris and his colleagues, with the assistance of the American Drug Enforcement Agency which had provided the leads and pushed the case, were able to work systematically to break up the organization that was engaged in the narcotics trade on Ios. It was by no means simple, but with the effective cooperation of the Greek and American authorities, the operation met with success. "At last, something positive!" he thought and boasted about it. He had worked systematically on the case for some time and had pulled it off.

But now he faced a new dilemma. He thought through the disappearance of the two men over and over, but could reach no conclusion. Logically, something about the case didn't seem right. Emver was hiding something even though he played dumb. Perdikaris decided to have Emver tailed to see what he was up to and who he was meeting. He had assigned the task to a new specialist. Was Emver on his own or were others involved? But nothing came out of it.

He was exhausted from his fatigue and the heat of the last few days. He slumped on his desk and gave himself up to sleep. A lethargy dragged him into the depths of the subconscious and then even deeper, into unexplored oceans. He found himself in a place enshrouded in fog. Around him, under him, and over his head. There was no sky and no earth. He was rolling on something, like a carpet, without weight, without resistance.

The fog surrounding him made it impossible to determine where he was. The time was not clear either. He had no sense of time or place. A cold sweat bathed him while at the same time, smoke suddenly started billowing up from under him. He panicked and tried to move away, but that too was impossible. A figure emerged from the cloud of fog and said something to him, but he did not understand or hear the words. He tried to get closer to the figure, but without success. Terribly anxious, he woke up in a sweat.

36

When the sun shines

let foolish gnats make sport,

But creep in crannies

when he hides his beams.

Comedy of Errors

Shakespeare

Peter, Hans and Otto dived boldly into the deep waters. The quickly reached the dark depths, reaching the place in the rock formation where the fissure leading to the narrow passage was. They entered into the passage where they could see the cave. From there, pushing against the water with their feet, they went into the underground caves and finally reached the point where they believed the shipwreck was.

Wearing special gloves and using tools for boring, they began to dig into the sand. They dug at a rapid pace and saw that there was something underneath the spot where they were digging. Suddenly they heard a deafening crash and the earth shook to its foundations. They found themselves sucked forcefully downwards as if by as whirlpool. Before they knew what was happening, they were pulled to the floor of the cave and engulfed.

37

His voice is as the sound of many waters.

Book of Revelation

New Testament

Startled and numb, Peter opened his eyes. His whole body ached and he felt a terrible discomfort. His feet and hands were totally numb. He was still in his wetsuit and mask and the oxygen cannisters were still on his back. But he couldn't move. Nor could he understand where he was.

He looked next to him and saw a fallen Otto on his side and, beyond him, Hans in a similar state. They appeared to be unconscious. He tried to recall what had happened and how they got there. But where were they? He looked all around, but it was dim and hard to make things out.

He thought he saw something move. And a figure, in fact, was approaching him. His heart began to pound intensely. It was something strange and he didn't know if what he saw was real. The strange figure neared him. It was seemingly a man, but except for his head and naked body, he couldn't make out clearly what it was. As he tried to get up, he saw that, from his mid-section down, the man had the body of a fish. It was a gorgon. "It's not possible. I'm hallucinating," he thought.

But no. The creature neared him and, without speaking, started to inspect him. Peter was terrified by the scene. He couldn't believe his eyes. What was that? Where was he? Was he inside the shipwreck or somewhere else? Impossible. He was hallucinating and soon he would wake up in the hospital. Maybe he had died and had passed over to the other side? "I must have died," he thought. "Maybe I am already navigating in another dimension."

But no. The creature was there before him. He opened and closed his eyes, but again, before he had a chance to move, the creature pressed his face against the mask. He was telling him something while at the same time a piercing sound shot through his ears.

Peter lost consciousness and passed out, his head dropping to his chest.

Hours later, he recovered. The strange creature again came close and, without making a sound, spoke inside Peter's head.

"We have been waiting for you for a long time. We have been trapped here for centuries, perhaps thousands of human years. We have become this way, just as you see us now. But we are alive! Over time, you will become like us."

"Where are you from and where are you headed? How did you end up here?" Peter said within himself, receiving an answer from the creature with the fish body, "Let's say we are Egyptians, but from Almitak in the zone of Orion. We are coming for a good purpose. Don't ask more. You will learn in time. When you recover, the others will explain. Right now, you need to recover."

After these words, he departed and Peter fell again into a torpor. In the strange, lethargic sleep into which he fallen, he saw a foreign land, one he had never seen before, and felt a strange fear within him. He was overcome by that fear. He couldn't recover. He was submerged and disabled.

The other two were in the same place, without having moved at all. The strange gorgon appeared again along with three others, observing up close the Germans who were unconscious and made no movement. They said something between them and then left, swimming into the depths of the cave.

38

I saw Eternity the other night

Like a great ring of pure and endless light.

The World

Henry Vaughan

The police officer was pulling out his hair. Now, aside from the Loumir and Vangos, the two who had disappeared, three others, this time Germans, had now been lost.

The Coast Guard had done a search, but without luck. They found no trace of the three Germans. Their friends made a statement and answered question at the police station, but nothing came of it. They repeatedly searched in the place where they had been, but found nothing. The sea had swallowed them up.

Dieter informed Peter's family, who arrived on the island to help with the search. So did the relatives of the other two. But the search ended up with nothing.

The parents of the Germans met several times with police chief Perdikaris, but they reached no answers about what happened to their sons. The situation itself was tense and their questions remained unanswered. They felt deeply disappointed, as they realized, even if they did not admit it, that they were not going to see their children again. It became clear that they were lost forever. How they were lost and how it happened were questions that continued to torment them.

The police chief, despite his good intentions and honest efforts, was unable to provide any convincing explanations. The German sailing friends said nothing about the treasure, Dieter was pressured not to mention it. *So the matter remained buried.*

After two weeks, and once the families of the vanished men had done their search as well, efforts ceased.

One version of what really happened was that perhaps some rock slide resulting from an aftershock had taken place on the day of their excursion and that that maybe was the reason that the unfortunate divers were trapped in the depths at the bottom of the sea. *In any case, despite the repeated search, nothing at all, not even a piece of rubber from their suits, was found.*

Dieter and Carla remained on the island, since Dieter finally found a house and bought it together with his lover. They informed their relatives that the wedding would take place on the island in a few months and invited them to come and join them.

Here ends the story: with Dieter and Carla in love with each other, with the Germans finally departing Ios for their homeland, with Andreas, Antonis and Haris staying on the island as before, and with police chief Perdikaris racking his brains to understand what the devil had happened with the loss of five persons in the waters of Ios: three Germans, one Greek, and one Albanian.

I would like to thank my old and dear friends Alex Philippides, for his positive input, and Perla Zerdevas, for her warm and encouraging remarks regarding the book.

SAILING THE WATERS OF IOS

The Story

An ancient shipwreck and its treasure lie hidden in the depths of the Aegean Sea, bringing to the enchanting Greek island of Ios the daring Peter and the urbane Dieter, two friends from Hannover, Germany.

They dream of getting rich. But as they soon discover, life holds many surprises.

Will they find what they are seeking? And what does the search for treasure mean for each?

Their magical trip strains relationships, but opens up new horizons, while a startling event marks the end of their quest.

Lydia Vassiliades was born and raised in Athens, Greece. Since her mother was a painter and actress and her father a publisher, she enjoyed the company from her early years of notable Greek painters, actors, writers, and poets.

After completing her studies in economics at Paris VIII, she worked as a journalist at the Athens New Agency until 2010, and for a number of Greek media, including the daily financial newspaper, *Express,* the newspaper *Dimosiografos*, the magazine, *Capital,* and a series on Greek Public Radio on Greek poets whose poems had been set to music.

She also served as editor-in-chief for the bulletin of the European Commission office in Athens, as well writing for numerous other media. Having broad cultural interests, she authored an opera libretto and wrote several song lyrics.

Sailing the Waters of Ios is her fourth novel and the second to be translated into English. Her other books *Chicago-Athens Athens-Chicago* (in English), *From Paris to St. Malo* and *Highgate Revisited.*

Made in the USA
Las Vegas, NV
14 July 2023

74720325R00090